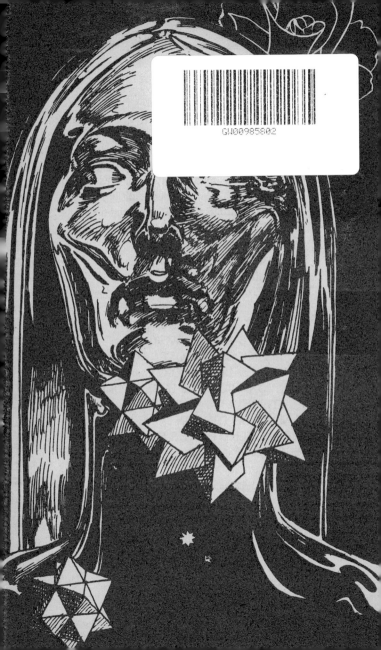

Tor Books by Roger Zelazny

DAMNATION ALLEY

Tor Books by Fred Saberhagen

BERSERKER BASE (with Poul Anderson, Edward
   Bryant, Stephen R. Donaldson, Larry Nivens, Connie
   Willis, and Roger Zelazny) (trade edition)
BERSERKER: BLUE DEATH (trade edition)
THE BERSERKER THRONE
THE BERSERKER WARS
A CENTURY OF PROGRESS
COILS (with Roger Zelazny)
THE EARTH DESCENDED
THE FIRST BOOK OF SWORDS
THE SECOND BOOK OF SWORDS
THE THIRD BOOK OF SWORDS
THE FIRST BOOK OF LOST SWORDS:
   WOUNDHEALER'S STORY (hardcover)
THE SECOND BOOK OF LOST SWORDS:
   SIGHTBLINDER'S STORY (hardcover)
THE MASK OF THE SUN
AN OLD FRIEND OF THE FAMILY
THE VEILS OF AZLAROC

ROGER ZELAZNY AND FRED SABERHAGEN

COILS

A TOM DOHERTY ASSOCIATES BOOK

COILS

Copyright © 1982 by The Amber Corporation and Fred Saberhagen

First Tor Printing: November 1982
Second Printing: June 1988

A TOR Book

Published by Tom Doherty Associates, Inc.
49 West 24th Street
New York, NY 10010

Cover art by David Lee Anderson
Interior illustrations by Ron Miller

ISBN: 0-812-55877-4
Can. No. 0-812-55878-2

Printed in the United States of America

0 9 8 7 6 5 4 3 2

ROGER ZELAZNY AND FRED SABERHAGEN

COILS

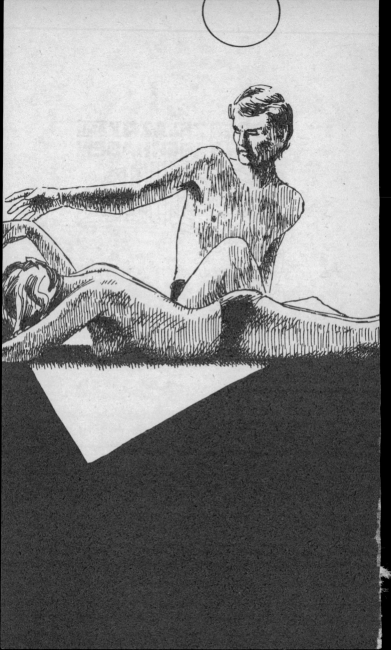

ONE

Clickaderick. Clickaderick.
Starboard, two degrees.
Click. Click.

. . . And through the half-built drowse-dream, words unlaunch a thousand ships, burn my topless towers, aluminum. Sweet, and fleeing . . . Fled now. What—

"You're a strange man, Donald BelPatri," they came. "Things have happened to you."

I did not turn my head. I feigned sleep as I sorted my senses. The world had slipped away again, as it sometimes does. Or had I? Still here, now, though, us, as I'd left us, but moments before. Here: The roof of my houseboat, *Hash Clash*, puttering along, maybe a kilometer an hour, through the mangrove channel that winds southwest along the flank of Long Key, about halfway down from Miami toward Key West. Warm, cool, light, dark. Flick, flick. . .

We were running on the new autopilot, a Radio Shack model, which matched information from the recently installed government navigational beacons along the waterway against its programmed-in map, seasoning the mixture with a little radar as a charm against collisions. The channel here was quite narrow, with places where two houseboats would be pinched in passing—which also meant it was sufficiently shady to make extended periods of summertime exposure comfortable. More than that. Pleasurable. And that was all I really cared about. But—

I did not turn my head to Cora right away; I just grunted. I had to do that much at least, because I could tell from her tone that she knew I was awake.

But my response was far from adequate. She waited silently for something better.

"A truism," I said at last. "Name three people to whom things have not happened. Name one."

"Well-educated," Cora mused now, as if she were dictating notes into a recorder. "Reasonably intelligent. Age about . . . what? Twenty-seven?"

"Give or take."

"Size, large. Though not yet deformed by excessive intake of Italian food." In the two weeks since we'd met, we'd developed a standing joke about our mutual fondness for pasta. It made a pretty way to keep the interrogation light. "Financial position—evidently secure. Ambitions . . ." Cora deliberately let it trail off.

"To have a good time," I supplied, still not turning.

With my eyes closed, the puttering of the engine

blended in my imagination with the chattering through the microcomputer of bytes of information. I didn't really trust the damned thing yet. If I did I could have passed from drowsiness into a deep, dark sleep, with it in charge of things. Then this questioning would have been avoided. Well . . . postponed, I guess. Sooner or later, though, I knew that it would be upon me. Cora had been working up to it for several days now.

"Which," she answered, "you have elevated to art-form status. Eyes blue. Hair dark and curly. Rugged features. A prejudiced person might even say 'handsome'. No visible. . ."

No, none quite visible. Under ordinary circumstances, that is. But that was why her voice had trailed off this time. The scars were well concealed under the famous dark and curly. She had discovered them about a week ago, one day when my head was in her lap, and had asked me about them. Suddenly, it seemed as if she had been nagging me continuously on the subject, and I wished to hell that she would stop.

I knew that if I told her bluntly to mind her own business, she would.

But, of course, I might never see her again after I did that. And I was discovering that I wanted very much to go on seeing her.

She seemed attracted to me on a deeper-than-summer-vacation level, and I. . .

I turned my head, resting it on folded forearms, looked at her. She was tall too, almost six feet, a long lithe body stretched out now on the beach towel spread on the houseboat roof. She'd taken off the top of her two-piece swimsuit, but the piece of fabric was in handy reach—in case of an emergency, such as perhaps a serious argument with me.

A basically cautious young lady, as might be expected of a schoolteacher. Basically lovely, too. Not a Hollywood face, by any means. Her dark hair was worn shorter than current fashion decreed, because, she said, it was easier to manage that way, and she had other things to do in life than take care of her hair . . . and the most basic thing about her, I was discovering, was that I didn't want to lose her.

"No visible reason for existence?" I suggested at last. Lightly, of course.

Cora shifted her position to meet my eyes.

"Tell me about where you grew up," she said. "From your speech I'd say it was somewhere in the Middle West."

Less danger there, or so it seemed. Danger? Did I really mean that? Yes, I realized. For an awkward moment I felt as if I were caught in a forked stick and held up for scrutiny. It hurt more in some places than others. Like my scars. I had always considered myself a private person beyond a certain point, and. . .

I was vouchsafed a glimpse of myself struggling in the pincers. Something was wrong. It was as if there were certain things I wasn't even allowing myself to ask. I saw, in my first moment's self-scrutiny in years, that there was a strand of irrationality woven through my being. But that was all that I saw. No way to approach it, let alone untwine it.

The thought passed as quickly as it had come, and I was glad of it. The ground was safer here.

"Upper Michigan," I answered. "A town so small

that I'm sure you never heard of it. Called Baghdad, of all things."

"As in '-on-the-subway?'"

"A long way from. Hiawatha National Forest isn't far away. A million lakes and a billion mosquitoes . . . What can I say? I'd a pretty typical small-town existence."

She smiled, for the first time in a long while.

"I envy that," she said. "I've told you something about Cleveland. I suppose your father owned the local lumber mill or whatever?"

I shook my head.

"No. He just worked in it."

I didn't feel much like talking about my parents, or even thinking about them, for that matter. They had been good people. Life in Baghdad had been idyllic. I'd led a sort of Huck Finn existence as a kid. Still, that was a long time ago, and I'd no desire to go back.

Another houseboat came into sight from around the bend and puttered toward us. My robot moved us a bit farther to starboard, providing ample leeway.

"I thought maybe you were living on some sort of inheritance."

Perhaps it was the sun that started my head to aching. I sat up. I rubbed the back of my neck.

"We didn't bring along any fishing gear, did we?" I said. "Damn! I was going to. Forgot."

"All right, Don, I'm sorry. It's none of my business."

The other houseboat had cut its engines and was coasting past us on momentum. The heads of two young men had just appeared at the same window on our side. Topless girl sunbathers were not that uncommon anymore, but ones as attractive as Cora evidently were. One of the boys said something that I tried to tune out. Uncomfortably, I moved to block their view as Cora started putting on her top. My head was throbbing now.

"No! Now, Cora . . . Damn it! Don't take it that way!"

"I'm not taking offense."

"But you're backing away from me. I can feel it."

"Backing? Or being pushed?"

"I. . ."

I stood up, but there was no place to go. The two leering youths were drifting on, and I looked after them almost hopelessly as they started their engines again.

I sat down, hanging my feet over the edge of the flat roof, my back to Cora. I drummed my heels on the fiberglass of the upper hull. The robot navigator mumbled its data in a madman's silence.

"Don, it's really none of my business where your money comes from. All I know is that you once told me that it amounted to eight thousand dollars a month being deposited in your bank account, and—"

"When did I tell you that?"

"A few nights ago. You may have been more asleep than awake," she said. "It sounded likely, though. You seem to lead a pretty comfortable life."

Beneath its carefully cultivated tan, I could feel my face turning red.

"You want to know where my money comes from?" I shouted. "Well, I don't!"

Why should she be able to make me feel like a child confessing some secret sin? I felt a mad urge to turn and strike her across the face.

There was a pause. Then, "You don't what?" she said, achieving a new note of puzzlement.

My throat was suddenly tight, my head splitting.

"I don't want to think about it!" I got out at last, the words coming in a rush.

Then I turned back to her—and suddenly my hand, which had been threatening to strike her a moment earlier now shot out and seized her wrist. I was unable to say another word, but I knew that I wasn't going to be able to let her go.

Her features took on a look of indignation which faded almost as rapidly as it occurred. As she stared at me, it was replaced by an expression of pity, concern.

"Don . . . Oh boy, you've got troubles—don't you?"

"Yes."

It was a relief to be able to say that much. Troubles? Yes, by then I knew I had troubles. I had no idea what they were. But troubles I had. I could see that. She'd helped to gain me that much of an insight.

"You're going to have to let my arm go," she said, trying to recover lightness. Her bra, imperfectly fastened, was threatening to fall off. "Here comes another houseboat."

I looked up. It was just rounding a gentle bend, eighty meters or so ahead. As I watched, my fingers relaxing until her wrist slipped free, a sun-reddened male face protruded on the pilot's side.

"Looks like Willy Boy Matthews himself," I said, surprising myself with what struck me as a humorous insight, coming totally out of left field.

I suddenly knew that some kind of internal crisis had just been passed, and I could feel myself half-choking with relief. I still had Cora with me. Whatever else, I felt that I wasn't going to break off with her.

"Willy . . .? Whatever made you think of him?" Cora sounded anxious to keep talking to me, about anything at all, while her hands were busy with refastening.

"I don't know. I guess the celebrities of yesteryear just pop up sometimes."

The face in the passing boat, seen now at close range, didn't really look much like that of the defunct revivalist preacher as I remembered him from screen and page. It was a gross, impressionistic resemblance more than anything else. When the mind really wants to be diverted, it seizes upon the handiest things.

"Now, do you want to tell me about your troubles?" she said. "I promise that nothing horrible will happen if you do."

I am not sure that I believed that, but I wanted to. For reasons not clear to me, I felt desperate, on the verge of tears. And it seemed a shame to waste all that trauma. Just a little more effort, I told myself, and I could get it all said. She would know as much as I did. We would be closer, where we had just been on the verge of moving apart. How could anything horrible come of it, despite the irrational forebodings which had come to dance upon my decks?

"All right," I said, looking out over the water to the places where it sparkled. "I don't know where the money comes from."

I paused a moment, hoping she'd say something. But she remained silent.

"So long as I don't push matters," I went on, "so long as I don't try to find out, everything will be okay. I just know it. It comes in on an EFT—you know, an electronic funds transfer—with no identification as to its source. About a year ago I did go into the bank and ask them how hard it would be to trace it. They said there was no way they could run it down on the information they had. Then I got sick for a couple of days, and I haven't thought about it since. But as long as I don't wonder about the money, I'm all right. Everything's fine."

Those last two words rang in my head. I had recited them as if by rote. I couldn't see how I had come to say them in light of the situation I had just described. Yet I had done more than that. For a long while I had believed them.

I raised my hand and rubbed my forehead, my eyes. The headache was still there. When I lowered my hand I realized that it was shaking.

Suddenly, Cora's hands were on my shoulders.

"Take it easy, Don," she said. "What I'd thought was that maybe you were getting some sort of disability payments. I mean, what with the head scars and all. But that's certainly nothing to be . . . ashamed of."

I realized that I *was* acting as if I were ashamed. I'd no idea why I should, though. Mostly now, I was afraid to think about it too much. I knew why now,

too. There really was something—unusual—about
the way I was set up in life. But far more unusual had
been my attitude toward it—for how long? I was
perspiring profusely now. There had to be something odd involved. Somehow, I knew that they
weren't disability payments. I didn't know what the
hell they were, and I didn't want to know. I realized
that I was afraid to find out. I was so damned scared
that I would do almost anything to keep from knowing. Yet—

Cora slipped down into a sitting position beside
me, extending her legs, long and tanned, feet dan-
gling. We both regarded the rippling waterway, al-
ternately dark and shiny as we slid from shade to
light, more Rorschach than magic mirror, I suppose,
for she saw nothing of my fears.

"I don't suppose it's anything actually sinister,"
she mused softly. Then, after a time, she added, "But
you said that your family isn't wealthy?"

I nodded, only half-hearing, now that some crisis
had passed. She had scored a sort of victory and we
both knew it, though neither of us could say what,
and I was only beginning to see how. For me, she
sang beyond the genius of the sea. I knew that I could
never go back to being exactly the same person I had
been only a little while ago. I shuddered, and then I
took hold of her hand. We continued to watch the
water, and the pain in my head subsided.

There was a moment of crystal clarity, and then I
could almost see the pine and the spruce towering
around us instead of the mangrove. I could smell
and hear the forest instead of the salt splashing
ocean fluttering its empty sleeves.

For the first time in a long while—years, I suppose—I wanted to go back home.

"Cora?"

"Yes?"

"Fly home with me and meet the family?"

Oh! Blessed rage for order. . .

TWO

Ticket? Ticket. . . ?
Ticket.
Something clicked. Not audibly. Something some-
how somewhere else.
Clicket. Click it. Ticklicket. Ti—
Spin. Advance and retreat. Pause. Pulse. Turn.
Again. The big, shiny bowl of alphabet soup was jiggled
before me. Facade. I dove through it to where the hand
that held the strings of power moved. Of course. One
will take me to another and that other to another still.
Back. Winding and pulsing. . .

The marina into which we took the *Hash Clash*
that afternoon had all the amenities, including
hookups for onboard computer phones. A lot of vacationing executives liked to have such devices
along on their boats.

I had lost every distressing symptom I had acquired earlier, though I was left with an overlay of almost pleasant fatigue and a lightheaded stupor of the sort I knew I could shake if I had to. No such need arose, however, and I was grateful for the anesthetization one's body or mind sometimes cleverly provides. A huge steak could complete the spell more than adequately. But business first, I decided.

"I might as well order the tickets now," I said, feeling a certain eagerness.

Cora smiled and nodded.

"Go ahead. I haven't changed my mind."

I went out and mated the simple plugs that connected us with the information networks of the mainland and the world. Then I returned to the other room, where I kept my unit.

There ought not to have been anything especially difficult or exotic about ordering the tickets. Essentially, it just amounted to my putting my personal information-processing equipment into contact with that of the airlines and the bank, along with my orders as to how many people were going where and when, and what class of service was desired. But—

It was after I'd taken care of the business. No reason then not to reach out and switch off the unit. But I didn't. Instead, I stared at the display screen, feeling a pleasant sense of accomplishment now that the ticket. . .

Ticket. . . ?

I drifted into a kind of reverie, I guess, first thinking about the ticket and what it meant, and then about the neat, smooth functioning of the machinery itself that made it all possible, and then. . .

It seemed that I heard Cora call to me once, but in a passive, general inquiring tone that hardly required a reply. I had a sort of waking dream then.

It was as if I were traveling along lines, bright and dark, moving at a vertiginous rate, as if I rode some crazy roller coaster—up, down, around and through—traveling back, back through some familiar territory, some landscape of the mind or spirit I might have visited in some previous incarnation, or yesterday in a moment of inattention. And there, there at the end of the line was a place where some of my life was stored away. Walls surrounded it, barring my entrance when I got there. I sought to pass them and silent alarms shook about me in my course. . .

"Don! Are you okay?"

I looked up and Cora was staring at me through the doorway. I managed a smile.

"I was thinking about home," I said, shaking off the dust of dreams, knuckling my eyes and yawning.

"For a second I thought you'd fallen asleep, or—"

"—freaked out?" I finished. "No such luck. I know you have to be fed occasionally. Get ready and—"

I suddenly realized that she was wearing a dark blue wraparound skirt and a red halter.

"Give me five," I said, "and we'll go ashore and hunt proteins."

She smiled. I shut off my terminal.

Going home. It still felt good.

Ticketderick.

In Detroit we changed planes for Escanaba, Upper Peninsula, on the northern shore of Lake Michigan. The bright lens of the lake, along the shoreline at least, was sprinkled with the confetti of summer sailboats—an almost electrical sensation for me.

Everything became feverishly familiar the farther
we penetrated into my pastoral past made present. I
kept pointing things out to Cora—landmarks, facts,
histories sprang to mind and tongue almost unbid-
den.

We picked up our rental car almost immediately
on landing, having brought no luggage other than
shoulder bags. We drove on Highway 41 north out of
the town along the shore. The sun struck the great
glass of the lake a glancing blow and waves raced
like fracture lines toward us. After a few miles, we
turned inland on state road G38, heading toward
Cornell. The dark green, shaggy horizon was comfortably near at hand. I sent my imagination on
ahead, flowing through, peopling the terrain.

"I still think we ought to have phoned," Cora said,
not for the first time. "In five years people change,
things change."

Five years. Was that right? Was it that long since
I'd been back? I'd given the number to her off the top
of my head, not really stopping to measure things
out. I hadn't left Florida at all last year—1994—or
the year before, so far as I could recall. Then, in '92
. . . I couldn't quite recall what I had done in '92.

"I'm nervous about meeting your family."

A road sign put Baghdad fifteen miles beyond
Cornell, and so did I.

I turned and smiled at her.

"You have nothing to worry about."

"I hope not."

"It'll be all right."

How could it be any other way? The closer we got
to Baghdad, the less concern I felt about the specifics
of what we were going to find when we got there. The

important thing was . . . I smiled . . . the important thing was Cora and me.

Cornell, small as it was, had evidently seen some changes in the past few years. Hardly anything about it struck me as familiar. But the road, and the tall trees closing it in on both sides—and the old railroad track, an occasional water tower, the placement of a faded billboard—felt crushingly familiar.

"That," I said, "is new"—the first words spoken by either of us in several miles.

The first gas station that we encountered on the outskirts of Baghdad was a small, weathered Standard, not the large new-looking Angra Energy that I recalled so clearly. There was a new sign, too, at the city limits:

BAGHDAD

POP 442

I drove on into town, slowing to the posted 30. There was only the one thoroughfare passing through town that qualified to be called a highway, and while in town it was the only way that really amounted to much of a street. The sideways leading off of it were unpaved, weed-lined, rutted and potted in places. Tin-roofed houses, some few with yards sporting vehicles pillared on concrete blocks, worn threshing and tilling gear, burned-out household appliances, collapsing sheds and partially dismembered felled trees, crouched as if to conceal worn shingles and flaking paint behind rough hedges, stands of hollyhocks and clusters of lilacs gone wild.

The real trouble was that this was not the main

street that I remembered. But then, perhaps at the other end of town. . .

Only we reached the other end of town with sickening suddenness, passed a final building and were back in the country again.

Pop 442.

It couldn't be *that* small. Surely, as a child, I'd had around me some semblance, if not of city life, then of life in a world where cities existed—not this utterly isolated backwater. I remembered . . . more than this. Where was the red brick school with the black iron fire escapes, the white church with the steeple, the theatre with the big marquee? Where was my parents' home?

Cora, from the way that I was driving, peering at everything, surely knew that something was wrong. Or perhaps she supposed that whatever had been wrong all along was now taking a new turn.

I braked, pulled as near to the ditch beside the narrow shoulder as I could and made a U-turn. No problem. There was very little traffic, even now, in summer. Nothing in sight. Slowly, I drove back to what would have to be called the business district. There were four stores—count 'em—and all of them were, behind old and weathered facades, utterly unfamiliar to me.

CAFE

Yes, a good idea, that. I parked the car—I could probably have left it in the middle of the street—and we got out and went in.

We seated ourselves at the counter, the only customers, and ordered iced tea. The day was warm. It probably didn't look strange that I was sweating.

"Do you know a BelPatri family, living around here?" I asked the tired-looking waitress with blue fingernails.

"Who?"

I spelled it out.

"No." She could have been the owner, one of the owners or a relative. She had an indefinable look of having lived here for many years. "There was a family named Bell, I think," she added, "over in Perronville."

"No."

We sat there drinking our tea. I watched a frighteningly experienced fly work his way into a glass case to explore the coconut topping on a wedge of something yellow and dry-looking. I did not want to look at Cora. I answered her small talk with monosyllables.

After I paid we went out and got back in the car, to drive slowly south. I stared up each of the ways that passed as side streets. Nothing. Nothing at all was right. There was nothing at all that looked as it should.

At the edge of town, I pulled into the Standard station and ordered gas. No recharge service here, I noted; few or no electric cars yet in the backwoods this far north, away from the Sunbelt and easy recharging. The new Angra station that I thought I remembered (I *did* remember!) had had a charger facility, though, hadn't it?

With the station attendant I again went through my futile questions about a BelPatri family. I spelled the name. Cora listened, giving silent, patient support. He'd never heard the name.

When we were back in the car, before I started the engine again, she spoke:

"Do you remember what sort of street your house was on?"

"Sure," I said. "The only trouble is, that memory is wrong."

I was shaken by the discovery—yes. But not, I realized, shaken as badly as I ought to have been. On some deep level, perhaps, I had known all along that the home I remembered, and the childhood, were elaborate lies. It had been important to come here and face the fact, though, and very important to have Cora with me when I did it.

I spelled it out a little more fully, as much I think for myself as for her:

"Sure, I remember a street, and a house. But they're not in this town. None of the streets that I remember are here, and none of the houses, and none of the people. And of the people and things that are here, I don't remember any. I've never been in Baghdad, Michigan, before."

There was a long silence. Then, "There couldn't possibly be two. . . ?" she said.

"Two towns with the same name, in Upper Michigan? Both just a few miles northwest of Escanaba, on the same road? The road I *do* remember, and what I remember fits. Right up to the edge of town. Then . . . It's as if something else has been—grafted in."

I did not know as I said it whether I meant that the graft was in geography or in my memory. Either way. . .

"And your parents, Don? If they're not here. . ."

Their images were still as clear as ever. But impersonal, as if they had never been closer to me than film or page. Mom and Dad. Great folks. I didn't want to think about my parents any longer.

"Are you all right?"

"No, but—" I realized that in some way I was at least better off now than I had been, back in Florida without a worry in the world. "Come back with me to Florida?"

Cora giggled a little, I suppose with partial relief at the fact that I was handling it so well.

"I don't think—I really don't think that I want to spend the rest of my summer vacation here."

I pulled out onto the familiar road. Good-bye, Baghdad, thief of my youth. You could have been Samarkand, for all I knew.

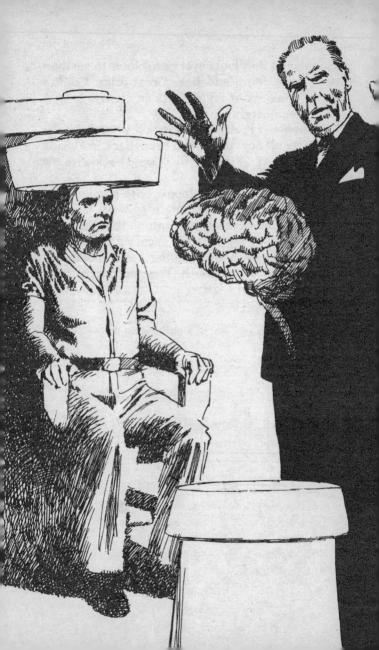

THREE

Sunset and evening star, horizon garlanded with
faded roses—

We had managed a quick connection down to Detroit and a close one for Miami. Cora did not want
the window seat, so I sat there watching star holes
get poked through the dark.

"You going to see someone when we get back?"
she asked me.

"Who?" I said, already knowing. "And about
what?"—knowing that, too.

"A doctor, of course. Someone who specializes in
things like this."

"You think I'm crazy?"

"No. But we know that something's wrong. If your
car isn't working right, you take it to a mechanic."

"And if thy right eye offend thee?"

"Nobody's asking you to play Oedipus. I'm talking
about a psychiatrist, not a psychoanalyst. It may be

29

something organic, a bone splinter pressing
somewhere—from your . . . accident—or something like that."

I was silent for a long while. I couldn't think of
anything better, but, "I just don't like the idea," I
finally said.

" 'There is nothing to do with such a beautiful
blank but smooth it,' " she said almost bitterly.

"Huh?"

" 'Sweet Lethe is my life. I am never, never, never
coming home!' Sylvia Plath," she said. "From a
poem about amnesia. You want to go on not knowing?"

"Count on an English teacher for a quotation," I
said, but I didn't like that last line at all.

I couldn't just forget about the trip to Michigan
and slide back into happy ignorance, I told myself.
No. And maybe, now that I knew, I could work
things out on my own. But then again I had a funny
feeling that perhaps I could slide back, dismiss all of
this and start drifting again, never, never, never
coming home. It scared me.

"Do you have any idea who's a good doctor for this
sort of thing?" I asked.

"No. But I'll damn sure find out."

I reached over and touched her hand. I met her
eyes.

"Good," I said.

Besides the houseboat, I owned a condominium
down in the Keys. But we checked into a hotel in
Miami, where the medical choices were considerably greater, and Cora got to work on the phone,
talking to an acquaintance of a friend of a friend

attached somehow to the administration of the medical school. Her theory was that you choose a doctor by finding out who the other doctors in the area go to with their own problems. A couple of hours after checking into the hotel I had an appointment with a psychiatrist, Dr. Ralph Daggett, set up for the next morning.

As if trying to prepare for the experience, my subconscious obligingly laid in a store of dreams that night. Willy Boy Matthews peered from behind a gas pump somewhere in the far north woods, warned me that the next time I rode an airplane I'd be in trouble, and then turned into a bear. Cora, having taken off all her clothes so she could better climb into my home computer and repair it, announced that she was really my mother. And still dreaming, I arrived at the psychiatrist's office to find a squat black monster waiting in ambush for me behind the desk.

The real presence, after I had duly awakened and shaved and had some breakfast, was not all that intimidating. Dr. Daggett was an engaging, outgoing man of about forty, built short and compact, husky rather than fat, like a somewhat enlarged, clean-shaven hobbit. On his desk before him he had the medical form I'd just filled out. He looked at it with a professional poker-face while we chatted a little about my reason for coming to see him. There wasn't much of substance on the form. As far as I could remember, I'd been disgustingly healthy all my life.

After giving the form to an aide to be fed into his office computer, the doctor peered into my eyes with a small light. He asked about headaches, of which my recent one on the houseboat had been a rare exception. He checked my reflexes, coordination and blood pressure. Then he had me seat myself in an uncomfortable chair where he affixed a stereotactic frame about my head and against the chair-back itself. The aide then wheeled in a machine, to take a CAH-NMR (computerized axial holography via nuclear magnetic resonance) scan of my brain. Unlike the earlier X-ray mediated mappings, this technique, which had come into use during the past several years, produced a holographic image of the organ upon a small staging area—somewhere out of sight, if you were squeamish; right before you, if you were not. I was glad to see that my physician was up to date, and I was not squeamish. While he had started out studying the image behind a folding screen, he removed it when I asked for a look.

A pinkish, grayish flower atop a fat stalk—I had never seen my brain before. Fragile-looking thing. Was that really what I was—Sherrington's "enchanted loom"—where billions of cells fired to weave me? Or was it a radio receiver through which my soul broadcast? Or Minsky's "meat computer"? Or—

Whatever it or I was/were, Daggett broke my train of speculations by removing his pipe from his mouth and using its stem as a pointer.

"This looks like a bit of scarring in the temporal region," he said. "Neat, though. Interesting . . . Have you ever had convulsions of any sort?"

"Not that I know of."

"Ever wake up and find your tongue badly bitten, your pants wet, muscle aches?"

"No."

He poked forward and the pipestem penetrated the image. I winced.

"Things can get very tricky down in the hippocampal area," he remarked. "Lesions there can do amazing things to memory, but—" He paused and made an adjustment. "Tell me more about what happened on this trip to Michigan. There! Your hippocampus looks okay, though . . . Go ahead. Talk."

He continued to play games with my brain-projection while I recited the entire story of the trip and its antecedents. Cora was present to confirm that these memories at least were accurate.

Finally, he threw a switch and my hovering brain-image vanished. Unsettling.

He turned to face me.

"I would like to try hypnosis," he said. "Have you any objection?"

I wasn't given much time to register one if I'd had one—a sign, I supposed, that my case was at least interesting.

"Have you ever been hypnotized before?" he asked.

"No, never."

"Let's get you into a more comfortable chair then."

He released me from the stereotactic unit and conducted me to a padded reclining chair, tipping it back about three-quarters toward the horizontal. A device within the chair itself detected my brain rhythms, matched its own gentle output to certain of them and then gradually amplified its output while at the same time introducing a subtle alteration. I could somehow sense the activity of the computer chip controlling this device. Its waves flowed through me like water and then I went unconscious, as I was supposed to, in a burst of white noise that flared inside my skull.

"How do you feel?"

Dr. Daggett's professionally intense face was bending closely over me. Cora was right behind him, looking over his shoulder.

"All right, I guess," I said, blinking and stirring.

It felt as if I had been asleep for a long while. It seemed as if there had been dreams, of the sort which just miss making it over into waking consciousness.

"What do you remember about Baghdad?" he asked.

There were still two sets of memories, one for the town that I had actually seen and another, tattered now and beginning to go dreamlike itself, of the Baghdad that until recently I had thought I genuinely remembered. And now I could vaguely sense, behind this dream-like fabric, another reality, shapes moving behind a curtain. I couldn't see yet what these shapes were. I told him this.

He asked me a few routine questions then, to make sure that I was at least fairly well oriented now, knew who I was (at least to the extent I'd believed I knew me when I entered his office) and what year this was and so on. He nodded at my answers.

"And for how long have you actually been living in Florida?"

The shapes behind the curtain shifted. Something vital was almost in view, but it slipped away again at the last moment.

I shook my head.

"I'm not certain," I said at last. "Several years for sure, though. What's been happening to me?"

"For one thing . . ." Daggett began, and then took his time about continuing, ". . .you told me on the medical history form that you had never had any serious head injuries."

The scars . . . Of course. Yet, oddly, they seemed to exist only in some other context. But it was obvious, logical and necessary to conclude that if I had them I'd gotten them from some sort of bashing.

"The scan is pretty conclusive, Don," he continued. "You've had at least one severe skull fracture. Do you recall anything about that now?"

The almost visible shapes came and went. Then they stayed away. I shook my head again. At least, now, I knew that there was something in my past to be discovered—and this felt like some kind of progress.

"And," he went on, "from what I've seen and heard so far, I'd say those old fractures aren't your only problem—not even the main one. In fact, it could be that they are not all that important in the etiology of your condition. There are indications here of deliberate abuse in the past, with some form of hypnotism, and probably drugs."

Why? I asked myself. It just seemed too improbable. For a moment, I doubted Daggett. But then he showed me the printout. Before I had awakened, he had run the results of his examination through his office computer terminal, which was connected to a large diagnostic data bank in Atlanta.

"My electronic colleague here concurs, you see."

I looked at Cora. She was biting her lip and staring at the printout as if it were a corpse.

"What does it all mean?" I finally managed.

He lit his pipe before answering.

"I think it means that someone has done a job on you," he said at last. "Whether the physical damage to your head was deliberate, I can't say. But the false memories you've been carrying around must have been intentionally implanted."

"Who?"

"Anything I said in answer to that now would be the sheerest speculation."

"Then speculate."

Daggett shrugged lightly.

"Certain governments have been known to treat people in such a fashion. But afterwards the people are not usually found living such a prosperous and carefree life." He paused. "You're native-born American, I'd say by your speech."

"I think so, too. Not Upper Michigan, though."

"Anything real about that period come back yet?"

For a moment, just for a moment, as he spoke, I thought I had hold of something, and then I almost had it. It was so close that I could nearly taste it. And then it was gone entirely. Out of reach. Kaput. A big piece of the truth, I just knew it, of the reality lurking right around the corner.

I made a face. I closed my eyes and knitted my brows. I clenched my teeth.

"Shit!" I said.

Daggett's hand was on my shoulder.

"It'll come, it'll come," he said. "Don't try so hard, just yet."

He turned away and began to scrape clean his pipe above a large ashtray on his desk.

"I could push harder with hypnosis," he stated.

"But then there's the danger of building a new con-struct, of trying so hard to find something that we make up a new falsehood to fill the need. No more today. Come back in three days."

"I can't wait three days. Tomorrow."

He put away the pipe and the scraper.

"The ice is broken," he said. "The best thing for a few days now will just be to give the truth, the real memories, a chance, so to speak."

"Tomorrow," I repeated.

"I don't want to push hard again that soon."

"Doctor, I have to know."

He sighed.

"All right," he relented. "In the morning. See the receptionist. She'll fit you in."

I looked at Cora.

"I suppose I ought to go to the police," I told her.

Daggett made a noise. I couldn't tell whether it was a snort or a chuckle.

"I am not saying that you should or shouldn't," he said slowly. "I would suggest, though, that if you can't tell the police any more than you know now, about all they'll be able to do is recommend you see a doctor."

The Catch-22edness was not wasted. The receptionist, who must have been used to every variety of emotion among the clientele, batted not an eyelash at my expression's inconsistency with lingering giggles. She fixed me up with the appointment and nodded me out. Exit pursued by clownsuited Furies tripping over one another's heels.

It was several blocks before the reaction set in.

"I'm scared, Don," Cora said.

She was driving. I was slouching and conjuring demons to wrestle with. They ignored me.

"I am, too."

And it was true, so far as it went. There was more, though. It was apparent from her manner that she was more frightened than I was. My deepest feeling was one I had not known for so long that now its touch was almost unfamiliar: I was beginning to get angry.

* * *

Angels? I was dead and in heaven, maybe? No. The musical tones were not really harp-like, and departed spirits shouldn't have the sour aftertaste of a six-pack in their mouths. I moaned and followed the notes back to the land of the living and the phone which was chiming. I had forgotten to switch the thing to Record before I'd gone to sleep, back when the demons might finally have stopped by. If they had, the final score was something like Demons Six, BelPatri Nothing. The clock flashed 8:32 and counting. I answered the phone.

The voice was sort of familiar. Yes. Daggett's receptionist. Something wrong about the way she sounded, though.

". . . We have to cancel your appointment," she was saying. ". . . Dr. Daggett passed away during the night."

"He what?"

"Dr. Daggett passed away. We . . . I found him in the office this morning when I came in. He'd had a heart attack."

"Sudden."

"Very sudden. He'd no history of heart trouble."

"He was working late, then?"

"Going over some patients' records. Listening to recordings. . ."

There was little more that she could tell me. Of course I wondered whether the recordings he had been listening to when he died had been mine.

I got up and washed up and dressed and brought back some coffee from the bathroom unit. Cora accepted hers gratefully and gave me a questioning look over the cup's rim. I told her what I had just learned.

She was silent for several heartbeats, then, "This thing is full of bad vibes," she said. "What— How— Hell! Do we start again with another doctor, or should we try to see his file on you?"

I shook my head.

"We won't get anything out of that office today," I told her, "and another doctor would just repeat what Daggett did yesterday—which seems kind of redundant. He'd said that things should start coming back to me now. I'd rather wait awhile and see. I think that he was right. I do feel different, as if something might be rearranging itself, clearing up, somewhere in my head."

"But—damn it!—we were so close—to something! This is almost too coincidental. Perhaps we ought to call the police. Let's tell them what he said and see if—"

"Hearsay and speculation," I said, "and from a psychiatric patient, at that. And even if they listened more than politely, there's really nothing to go on. A heart attack's a heart attack. He wasn't done in with a blunt instrument, or anything like that. We have nothing for the police. They have nothing for us."

She took a drink of coffee, set her cup on the bedside table.

"Well, what do you want to do?" she said then.

"Head down for the condo in Key West," I answered. "The bank should be getting in my next payment the day after tomorrow. We can just relax and wait for the therapy to take its course."

"Relax?" she said, swinging her feet over the side of the bed and sitting up. "How can we relax now, knowing as much as we've learned?"

"What else can we do?"

"We can wait for things at his office to settle and then try to see Daggett's records on you. He might have recorded more than he told us."

"We can check that out by telephone in a day or so, from my place. Get dressed and let's go get some breakfast—unless you'd rather eat here. Then we can get our stuff together and check out."

"No," she said, brushing her hair back with a forceful gesture. "I mean, yes to the breakfast—and no to the checking out."

"Well, get ready then," I said, turning away. "We can discuss the rest while we eat."

We wound up with a compromise. We would hang around for the rest of the day and stay over that night. We would try to get at my records that afternoon. If nothing came of it, we would be on our way in the morning.

Nothing came of it.

That is to say, Daggett's office was closed. The answering service could not or would not reach his family. I could not get hold of his receptionist. We finally got in touch with his nurse. She told me that there was no way I could get what I wanted right away. Psychiatrists' records, because of their sensitive nature, were sealed at the time of the physician's death, until a patient's new doctor requested them or a judge issued an order for their release. She was sorry, but—

Nothing came of it, on that front. However. . .

"Let's get a court order," Cora said.

"No," I replied. "I don't want to bring any more people into this than necessary. I kept my promise. We waited. We tried. Tomorrow we check out."

"Without learning?"

"It'll come back. I know it will. I can feel it now."

"You felt Baghdad pretty strongly, too."

"That was different."

"Oh?"

It was a rough evening. To top it off, the demons came back for another round, bearing armloads of nightmares. Mercifully, most of them faded in morning's light, save for the final war-dance of horrors around the Angra Energy pump while the earth opened before me as a fat man minced a gigantic holo of my brain with a blazing axe. All the little things that make sleep an adventure.

Cora was not overjoyed at our departure, but I'd kept my part of the bargain and she would not give me one up on her. A light rainfall pursued us much of the way as we drove on down. Pathetic fallacy. We were neither of us in good humor by the time we got there.

Once we were settled in at my place she started talking lawyers again. Didn't I have a local attorney I trusted, one who could pursue matters from here?

"No," I lied, because I was sure that Ralph Dutton, who I sometimes ran into, would handle it for me.

I simply did not want to go that route and I was sick of hearing about it. She wouldn't let it rest, though. I felt that anger again, this time turning toward her, and I didn't want it to come out. I told her that I did not care to talk about it any more, that I was getting another headache and that I wanted to be alone till it went away. I excused myself then to take a walk.

I wound up at a bar where I sometimes had a few. It was near Ernest Hemingway's old house. Did Hemingway really steal a urinal from another bar, I wondered, rip it out and take it home with him to make into a watering trough for his cats?

Jack Mays stopped by as I sat there drinking a beer. Big, freckled, always grinning, blond hair sunbleached nearly white, he had a perpetual schoolboy air about him which many people found engaging on first encounter. He was the most completely unserious person I knew. He was often in trouble, though there was nothing really malicious about him. He was basically a pleasure-seeker and, like me, he received a monthly deposit in his account. Only he knew where his money came from. His parents kept putting it there on the condition that he never return to Philadelphia. Jack and I had always gotten along well. It might be that he thought my situation was similar to his, if he thought about it at all. On those rare occasions when I hung one on, I liked to have him around, because he could hold a lot more booze than I could and still function, and he would keep an eye on me, keep me out of tight situations.

"Don!" He slapped me on the shoulder and sat down on the next stool. "It's been a while! You been away?"

"Yeah. Traveling a bit. What about you?"

"Got it too good here to want to leave," he said, slapping the bar. "Hey, George! Bring me one of those!"

"Got a couple of girls banked up with me," he continued. "You'll have to come by later. Fix you up."

His beer arrived, and we sipped and talked. I didn't tell him my troubles, because he's not the sort of person you tell your troubles to. He's great at small talk, though, which was exactly the size I felt most like dealing with at the moment. We talked about mutual friends, about fishing—which we sometimes did together—about politics, movies, sports, sex, food, and then started on around again. It was a relief, it was such a relief, not thinking about the things that bothered me most.

Before I knew it, it was getting dark. We had something to eat then—I forget exactly where—and stopped in another place afterwards for a couple of more drinks. My head was swimming by that time, but Jack still seemed in great shape and kept up the steady flow of talk till we turned up the walk to his place.

Then we were inside and he was introducing me to a couple of girls, turning on some music, mixing drinks, more drinks. After a while we danced a bit. After another while I noticed that he and the tall one, Louise, had disappeared, and I was sitting on the sofa with Mary, my arm around her shoulders, my drink in my lap, hearing the story of her divorce for the second time. I nodded occasionally and kissed her neck every now and then. I am not certain that she was interrupted in her narrative by this.

After an even longer while, we were in one of the bedrooms in a state of undress, hugging. Later still, I woke up briefly with vague memories of having disappointed her, and I noticed that I was alone. I went back to sleep.

I did not feel well the next morning, but I remembered that Jack's bathroom was a virtual pharmacy, and I staggered off after a mess of remedies.

As I was gulping vitamins, painkillers, stomach settlers and a muscle relaxant I had come across, a shape suddenly moved into sight from beyond that magic curtain. At first, I didn't quite realize what it was. When I did, I paused in the midst of rinsing my mouth, afraid that I'd choke myself.

There was a noise in the hall. I spit out the mint-flavored stuff, rinsed the bowl and stepped outside.

It was Jack, wrapped in an orange and yellow beach towel, coming to the john.

"Jack! I used to work for Angra Energy!" I told him.

He just stared for a moment, bleary-eyed, and then, "Commiserations," he said and went on in.

He'd been to almost all the Ivy League schools. You can always tell.

I went out to the kitchen and made coffee. I got dressed and I drank some orange juice with a raw egg and Tabasco Sauce while it finished brewing. Then I took a cup out onto the porch.

The sun was several meters above the horizon, but the morning was still somewhat cool. A breeze full of moisture and salt reached me. Birds were questioning one another in the bushes on both sides of the house.

It bothered me when I thought about Cora, but in some ways I felt better than I had in a long while. I was remembering, and that pushed everything else out of my mind. . .

Yes. I had worked for Angra. Not as a roughneck, a driller, or anything like that. It had not been out in the field. Not manning a station . . . I almost said to myself 'nothing technical', but something told me that that was not strictly true.

I took another swallow of coffee.

Data processing, maybe. I did know something about computers. . .

Somewhere in a central office, or laboratory, something . . . Yes, a lab of some kind. That might be it.

Then, for just a moment, I had a vision—whether memory, imagination or some combination thereof, I could not say for certain—of a door, a door paneled in old-fashioned frosted glass. It was swinging shut, leaving me on the outside. Its black lettering read COIL DEPARTMENT.

Of course, electrical coils of wire, inductances, still played a part in some devices such as relays, not having been superseded by the chip and the microchip. . .

How about this, I suggested to myself, for a scenario? A laboratory accident, resulting in a head injury, accounting for the scars. Then false memories implanted, covering years of my life, a step somehow necessary to cover up the liability, the responsibility, of some people in the company? And then a pension, to keep me away and quietly secure?

But a lot of people were in accidents of one sort or another—and I'd never heard of anything so exotic happening to anyone as a result. Big companies can afford to make settlements. They do it all the time.

No, it didn't sound quite right.

But I could feel that there was more coming. I finished the coffee and rose. I set the cup on the railing.

It was time to go and square things with Cora. At least I had some good news.

I entered my place and called out:

"Cora?"

No answer.

Well, it was understandable. I expected her to be miffed. I'd only said that I was going for a walk. She'd probably done some worrying, too. It made me feel a little more rotten. I formed instant resolutions to do all sorts of nice things for her—dinner and flowers and. . .

"Cora?"

I looked into the next room. Empty. Could she have gone and checked into a motel? Really mad? Well. . .

MESSAGE WAITING said the light on the phone/computer screen, right where it would be if someone had phoned—or left. My stomach clenched itself and a taste of coffee came into my mouth.

I crossed the room and touched the switch. The screen read:

> DON —WHAT WITH ONE THING AND ANOTHER,
> TIME THAT I MOVED ON. ITS BEEN GREAT
> SUMMER FUN BUT WE SHOULDNT TRY TO MAKE
> ANYTHING MORE OF IT.
> YOUR'S IN MEMORY, CORA

I looked through the other rooms with sufficient thoroughness to be certain that all of her things were really gone. Then I returned, sat down, stared at the screen again. On a display screen, of course, there is no way of checking handwriting, no signature to scrutinize. But any English teacher who switched her apostrophes around like that. . .

I was almost surprised by my reaction. I felt neither depression nor hysteria, not sadness, not fear. Something else, altogether.

My mouth was dry, though, and I opened the refrigerator and grabbed the only cold drink in sight, a can of beer, flipped the lid open and drained it in a short series of gulps.

My hand holding the empty can was shaking slightly, partly doubtless with hangover, but partly from fresh adrenalin. The adrenalin was from anger, not from fear. I had almost forgotten what it felt like to be this angry.

My fingers could move under my control with perfect ease. Why not? And yet, to a part of my mind, this seemed an oddity. Later, later . . . Think about that later. I watched the empty can crumple in my fingers like a flower.

The use of muscles seemed to clear the way for the use of other things. Intelligence, I hoped, was one of them. But not the only one. . .

Staring at the computer screen, I tried to see or not-see Cora's fingers on the keyboard, typing that message. The timing of the arrival of the bits of data at the CPU. . .

Intellectually, I had no clear idea of what I was doing. But at some deeper level I knew that I was seeing into the computer, probing its electrical life. It was a feeling akin to the half-dazed empathy I had in recent days felt for the Radio Shack navigator on the houseboat.

The shock of the discovery, or re-discovery, of this power in myself was deadened by my greater need. I could not find Cora's fingers. Those of a stranger had been there. . .

I had to switch to thinking now, to get any further. Adrenalin wasn't much help for that, and even my new-found ability stopped here. I cursed my quarrel with Cora, my leaving her alone to be attacked, kidnapped. I had only come back to Key West because it felt like my home ground, the place to make a last stand—not, as I thought she might have believed, because my money was due to come in today at the bank. . .

The bank.

In a flash, I saw again the old-fashioned door of frosted glass, swinging shut, as I had seen it in my reverie. COIL DEPARTMENT wasn't quite right, though; it was dream-language, the language of my unconscious, for something I had named in secret years ago, for my thoughts only.

The bank.

I went out of the condo and got into my car. I drove to the bank, pulled into the lot there. I parked in a spot shaded by a coconut palm.

I looked at my watch. The money was due to arrive at mid-morning—in the form of electrical impulses, flowing through the slender fiberoptic cables that brought information into and out of the Keys, cables slung under the same long bridges the cars and trucks traversed.

It had grown hot, humid. I left the motor and air conditioner running (nobody looked at you for that anymore, as they might have before solar power came on so fast—solar power and Angra Energy) and I leaned back in the seat and closed my eyes.

The computer inside the bank was a whole city, as compared to the small electronic outpost I had at home. But it was a city logically laid-out, with well-marked thoroughfares.

Hour by hour, minute by minute perhaps, I was remembering more. My mind reached for the bank's computer. The Coil Effect began.

FOUR

Ticketderick, and outward, into the magic city of light and darkness . . . Rivers of cold electronic fire flowing about geometric islands, passing under bridges, halting at dams, trickling here, surging there . . . Lights blinking like pinball displays . . . A roar, a whine. . .

I made my way through to a still place where I could survey the entire prospect, dipping a finger here, touching a pylon there, to sense the echoes of the data pulsing by. Gates opened and closed, neutral transactions flashed past like freight cars . . . No, no, no . . . Time was suspended. And even if it were not, it was so pleasant to be back . . . I could wait. If my body died right now, I almost felt as if I would continue to exist within the great machine which surrounded us. Ticketderick. . .

Stop. Slow. Freeze. Enlarge. Expand.

Yes.

I had hold of it. There, the symbol-chain bearing my monthly stipend: 1111101000000, with my name on it. I shepherded it into my account. Immediately, a verification of receipt bearing the same coding sprang phoenix-like from that crackling nest, took flight along the line of power my credit had come in on. . .

I tagged it, hooked onto it, followed my name. Along the chain of cabled highways, I knew at another level, built upon piers, island to island, through copper and fiberoptic connectors snaking in conduits at their sides, to the Miami clearing-house, passing through another, larger city of lights, murmurs all about me, then racing on, up, down, around, through, terminal to terminal, Atlanta, New York, New Jersey, and then. . .

Angra Energy, home office, New Jersey.

Yes. Of course. But I had had to know for certain.

I dove. I surfaced at the Stock Exchange, wheat futures beating all about me in soothing pulses. Something was coming back. . .

I was seven years old. I was sitting on the floor in the sales and service center Dad and Mom ran in El Paso. As other kids did with other toys, I was talking to an old computer, a 1975 model, which was off-line for repair but active for diagnosis. "What's wrong?" I said to it. "Why are you glitching?" There followed something like a burst of static in the center of my head and I twisted into its city of lights, only some of them were not burning. There, there, there—and there! I saw the pattern exactly as I had seen it that day. That had been the first time I had coiled into one. I—

The other world—the slower, less vivid one—intruded. I became dimly aware that someone was standing beside my car in the bank's parking lot, looking in at me. I did not want to go back to that place yet, but I knew that I must. Shrugging off commodities, I coiled back into my head and regarded the person who stared.

She was small, dark-haired, rather pretty, partly Oriental. She had on a white pants suit. She was staring.

She was someone I knew I should know.

I rolled down the window.

"Don, are you all right? You do not look well."

For a moment, I wondered whether she was some extrasensory leftover. But no, she had a name and substance to go with it. Ann. Ann Strong, I recalled. Nothing else, but I could use that much.

"Better than I've been in some time," I said. "What are you doing here, Ann?"

She smiled again.

"I see that you remember me, at least," she said. "I was not sure that you would."

I smiled.

"I'm not a total wreck," I said, and something else came to me. "How do you like the flowers?"

"So many and so lovely," she replied. "So pure their—colors."

Something special about her . . . "Colors" was not the word she had been about to use. I could just feel it. Something else. She had a special liking for something about flowers, but that was not it. . .

"Have you been in town long?"

"No." She shook her head slightly. "I'm barely arrived. You like this place?"

"I've grown fond of it."

"I can see how you would. But surely there must be more diverting things to do than to sit in the parking lot of a bank?"

"Unless one is waiting for Angra's conscience-money to come in," I said casually, partly just to try it out and partly because I had begun to suspect a connection.

She frowned. She puckered her lips.

"Tsk, tsk," she went, shaking her head slowly. "Hand and bite. Old saying."

"If I have to bite," I said, "it will be more than a hand."

"Why this rancor, Don?"

"Why are you here?"

"I had just gone to the bank to cash a check when I noticed a familiar face."

"All right," I said, "and perhaps well-met. May I drive you anywhere?"

"I was going to have something to eat next."

"I know a good place. Come on."

She got in. I drove out onto the road and turned left.

"Vacationing, then," I said.

"Sort of."

Something about her, something about her . . . Warning bells were ringing in the back of my head. It was as if I had already known whatever was the matter, but that something was holding the knowledge back from me. Not important, I decided. Not ultimately important, anyway. Somehow, Angra had to do with the gap in my life and with Cora's disappearance because of her connection with me. It just seemed that it had to be so. I was going to go up to New Jersey very soon and make a lot of noises. I was going to look up people who were only dark outlines now, walking through the mists of my memory. The names would come, the faces would come. I would find them. I would make them talk. They would give Cora back to me or I would do . . .

something. Something violent or revelatory. Or both. I no longer really had a choice.

I pulled into the parking lot of a small diner I sometimes frequented. It was an off-hour. Probably wouldn't be crowded.

We got out. I almost took Ann's hand, fluttering near my own, as we moved toward the door. I didn't know why. I caught a sudden aroma of hyacinths.

We found a small table in a corner and I suddenly realized I was famished. Conch soup, salad, lots of beef, iced tea, Key Lime pie—I ordered them all. She took a salad and a tea. Watching her, I became certain that I had known her during my employment at Angra. But in what capacity? I simply could not recall.

"It is good that you are happy here," she said, after a time.

"I've been happier."

"Really?" Her eyes had widened, and I thought I detected a momentary flush in her cheeks. But that was only for an instant. Her face hardened then. "But you will certainly have your joys returned. Things come back."

I seemed to smell roses.

"One can never be certain," I said.

She glanced down at her plate, speared a bit of lettuce.

"Some things can be relied upon," she stated.

"Such as?"

"Cooperation with those in power produces predictable results."

"These days one does not even know how to begin."

"You are troubled."

"Yes."

"You say you like it here."

"Yes. But I'll be leaving soon."

She met my eyes.

"That is not how to begin," she said.

"You know a better way?"

"Any way that avoids rash actions is better."

Several mouthfuls later, I said, "I wish I could show you around some later, but I have to catch a plane in awhile. New Jersey."

I watched her face as I said it. I wanted her reaction. There was an odor of jasmine in the air.

Her expression did not change as she said, "Don't be silly, Don. That comes under the heading of rash actions."

"What would you have me do, then?" I asked her.

"Go home. Stay there," she replied. "Sooner or later, someone will get in touch—"

"All right!" I said. "Let's level! You know more than I do. Where is she?"

She shook her head.

"I do not know."

"You know what is going on."

"I know that you are remembering things better forgotten."

"It's too late to do anything about that. And I am not going to sit at home and wait for the phone to ring."

She placed her fork upon her plate, raised her napkin and patted her lips.

"I would not like to see you harmed."

"Me neither," I said.

"Then do not go to New Jersey. Something bad will happen to you if you do."

"What?"

"I do not know."

I growled and she rose quickly and turned away.

"Excuse me," she said.

I was on my feet and moving after her. But several steps took her to the Ladies' Room and on into it. I hesitated.

Our waitress was passing just then with a carafe of coffee. I halted her.

"Is there another exit to the Ladies' Room?"

"No," she said.

"Any windows?"

She shook her head.

"Just four green walls."

"Thanks."

I went back to the table and finished my pie. I got a cup of coffee after the iced tea was gone.

A gray-haired woman went into the Ladies' Room. A little later, when she emerged, I approached her.

"Excuse me," I said. "Was there a small Oriental lady in there, in a white pants suit?"

She looked at me and shook her head.

"No. Nobody else."

I returned to my table and left a tip. While I was paying my bill at the register, I seemed to hear Ann's voice:

"Do not go," it said. "You think you have troubles now. At least you are still alive. Stay home. Bait not the tiger."

I looked all around, but she was nowhere in sight. I could almost feel her presence, though.

"Unfortunate," I said, under my breath. "What did you do—cloud my mind?"

I seemed to hear her laughter, mingled with the odors of a flower garden.

FIVE

I returned to the condo to change my clothes and toss the shaving kit and a few other things into a flight bag. I saw that there were no new messages in my unit when I approached it to broach the matter of a shuttle flight and a Miami to Philadelphia connection. There were no hitches, and the shuttle was due to depart in forty-five minutes. I locked the place up, got back in my car and headed for the airport. Ann's ghostly voice did not haunt me again, though I kept expecting to see her every time I turned a corner.

The long flight, I decided, would be just what I needed for sorting out a lot of new thoughts.

I parked, went in and verified my arrival at the desk. I was given a boarding pass, and since I had a little time I bought myself a cup of coffee and took it

with me to the waiting area. For the first time since I
had awakened, nothing was pressing upon me. I had
a few minutes before boarding in which to relax. I
settled back into a chair and took a hot gulp.

Ticketderick. . . ?

Relaxing. . .

Ticketderick.

I closed my eyes and I could feel the pulsing network of electronic activity around me. I guess it is
almost omnipresent these days, but especially con-
centrated in certain places, airports among them,
with data-processing gear all over the place.

"Hello," I said. "You are soothing," *and my mind
was massaged by the passing pulses. I thought of nothing. I coiled not, nor did I read. . .*

After several minutes, I withdrew from the flow. I
drank more coffee, and I stared out the windows at a
taxiing plane upon the runway. I felt better. Between Jack's medicine chest and a good lunch, all
traces of the hangover had fled. My mind was beginning to work as it had not worked in ages. Despite
Ann's warning, I began feeling a small confidence in
the success of my mission.

I did not want anything that they had, save for
Cora. The only reason that I could see for their having taken her was that they were somehow irritated
at my getting my memory back. They wanted some
hold over me in case I remembered something
damaging to them. I would be glad to promise to
keep my mouth shut about anything I remembered,
if they would just let her go.

How did they know that I had remembered anything I shouldn't have?

Baghdad was the first thing to come to mind. Perhaps I had been under surveillance. Or perhaps a big red light went on on a board somewhere if I bought a ticket for Michigan. Or if a psychiatrist ever ran a profile on me through a major medical bank. Or perhaps the *Hash Clash* and my condo were bugged. Or—Any number of possibilities came to mind. It did not really matter which had served to send the alarm. The fact was that they had suspected I recalled something they'd rather have forgotten.

What?

I strained. There were all sorts of images of me doing things with computers, but they were still too vague. They had wanted Cora for leverage, and now I wanted that memory for counterpressure—just in case my word wasn't good enough. I hoped the memory would return to me on the way up. If it did not, I would just have to try to bluff it. They were frightened or they would not have acted. That might be in my favor.

Even then, I was not overly concerned for my physical safety. After all, they could have killed me a long time ago had they so desired. Yet they had gone to extreme lengths to provide an alternative, damaging only my ability to recall some things.

The plane came to a stop outside and the passengers disembarked. A few minutes more passed, during which some luggage and freight was unloaded. Then the plane's interior was being cleaned and the tanks filled.

Shortly thereafter, an attendant entered the area and announced that passengers could begin boarding.

I rubbed my eyes. There was something wrong about the attendant.

I looked again. The man had visible, protruding fangs, and there was a greenish cast to his complexion. Was it some sort of gag? The other passengers took no heed of it and were beginning to move in that direction. I raised my bag and did the same. If it didn't bother them—

I must have been staring, though, as I passed, for he grinned at me as he inspected my boarding pass—a truly ghastly sight. I went on past, shaking my head. My times were definitely out of joint.

I froze as soon as I stepped out of the building. The plane had vanished. In its place stood a giant, old-fashioned hearse, with dark wooden coachwork and black curtains. It was hitched to a team of huge black horses adorned with sable plumes. I uttered some incoherent noise.

People elbowed past me and proceeded on to board. The horses snorted and tapped at the runway with their hoofs. I turned away. I couldn't board that thing. I knew that I would die—

Ticketderick?

I closed my eyes, blocking out the sight. I opened my mind. Sanity and consistency prevailed within the electric city of lights which surrounded me. These were defenses against evil visions.

A moment, another pulsebeat or two for it to restore me. . .

I lowered my head and opened my eyes again. Good, solid concrete, yellow lines painted upon it. . .

Follow the yellow concrete path. . .

I began walking.

I bumped into a lady and apologized. I had to look up as I did it.

We were at the foot of the ramp, but the vision had remained constant.

The vehicle was unchanged. I was about to board a glossy death-wagon. I had begun to discover the truth about myself, and now I was being warned against continuing.

I think that I turned away again, ready to examine alternatives to this trip. But then I thought of Cora, the reason I had to make it, the reason I had to board here, no matter what the thing looked like.

I reached out and put my hand on the rail, my eyes clenched shut. One step at a time, I mounted.

When I reached the top, I heard a surprised female voice say, "Is something the matter?"

"Yes," I replied. "I have a terrible fear of flying. Would you please help me to a seat?"

"Sure. Here."

I felt my arm taken. She guided me. I blinked my eyes open twice, for quick orientation.

The interior was filled with leering ghouls and monsters; it was illuminated by a flickering and baleful candlelight. I dared not look at the woman who guided me for fear of seeing the triple goddess and knowing I was gone, passed over, taken.

I found a place for my bag beneath the seat before me. Everything *felt* normal. Whatever the situation, it did not seem to apply to tactile sensations. I located the ends of my seat belt and clasped it about my middle without looking. I knew what I would see if I were to look—namely, that it had become a

serpent. Knowing this and seeing it were two different things, however. I had known what the interior
here would look like before I'd blinked myself a pair
of glimpses moments ago. But the knowledge in
itself was several degrees less gut-wrenching than
the primary experience. I realized that I was far
from rational at the moment, and this knowledge in
itself was somehow comforting. After all, I had un-
dergone a psychiatric treatment which had stirred
the depths of my being. It had produced results on a
rational, practical level. What I was undergoing
now, I told myself, was doubtless some sort of reaction by all the forces of unreason in my subconscious. Yes, cling to that, I decided; it puts it all onto
the plane of mental health as a kind of balancing of
the books. When it's all over—

Plane? Plane. We were moving. On one level, I
knew that we were turning, taxiing. On another, I
heard a mighty neighing sound and a clatter of
hoofs. The wagon jolted from side to side, the coach
wheels creaked and clattered.

Ticketderick.

Yes, again. Dive into the smooth flowing operations of the systems all about. Here they were simpler than in the terminal, but a few tiny lights of
rational structuring. Yet I held them and flowed
with them, entering a kind of trance-like state, cir-
cuiting through each functioning level over and over
and over again.

I held with it, moving in my own small world of
light through a sea of darkness. I was able completely to ignore everything about me for a timeless
span until the address system came on and the cap-

tain announced that we were about to land at
Miami. I knew that that was what he said, but on
that other level I heard the chimes as a brazen gong,
followed by the voice of Orson Welles, announcing
that Donald BelPatri was about to be dropped into a
boiling pit where he would remain until the flesh
was flensed from his bones. I almost screamed then,
but I bit my lip and clenched my hands till the
knuckles cracked.

We landed and finally came to a stop. The pressure suddenly vanished. Had my id taken a coffee
break, given up now that I was safely arrived? I
opened my eyes and saw normal people unfastening
belts and picking up bags. I did the same quickly.
Everyone near me made a point of avoiding my gaze.
I thanked the stewardess again on the way out and
made my way into the terminal, unflensed.

Inside, I located my gate, got another boarding
pass, visited the Men's Room, found a drink
machine and gulped two icy Cokes in rapid succes-
sion. I returned to the boarding area then and took
the seat nearest to the entrance tunnel. I wanted to
have everything possible in my favor in case of a
recurrence of my hallucinations. I performed all of
these acts on as basic a motor level as possible,
keeping my mind from everything but what my
body was doing. But once I sat down the thoughts
began to ooze again, at a higher level.

Had what might have been a mere anxiety reaction to my mental readjustments and Cora's disappearance been forced to such graphic, paranoid
levels by virtue of the fact that an actual menace had
been made apparent? I had not studied that much

psychology in college, but it seemed possible, given the extreme stresses to which I had been subjected.

College? I suddenly realized that I had attended a university. Where? Denver . . . ? That seemed right. I hadn't finished, though, hadn't taken my degree . . . Why not?

Blocked again, but left with a feeling that Ann had had something to do with it, with my leaving school. I had known her that long ago.

Ann . . . What was her weakness? What was her strength? She 'iad both, in unusual proportions. It seemed important that I should recall what they were, but I was blocked here, also.

I pushed hard. Harder. If my memories of Ann were closed to me, what about Angra? Angra Energy, my erstwhile employer . . . Computers. Me and computers. I wasn't an ordinary programmer or systems analyst or anything like that, though. I worked with them in a special capacity—very special, very valuable to Angra—using, yes, my unique sensitivity to the machinery itself, to the machinery and its functioning. I was too valuable for them to waste, even when I was no longer of immediate use. There was always the possibility that they might need me again one day. And so—

The announcement that we would be boarding in five minutes broke through my thoughts, scattered them. I had gained a little more, however. If I could just remember some of the details and some of the people involved. . .

Had the announcement served as a cue for the neurosis brigade to make its entrance, stage-left? Nothing had changed, but everything had changed.

The pressure was back. A before-the-storm feeling, a feeling of imminent doom, was crowding in around me again. I could feel my grip on rational thought-processes loosening. . .

But I'd been through it once and had survived. And this would be the last time. I swore that I would board no matter what. I rehearsed all of my defenses. I coiled into the fluctuating systems which surrounded me, into the flight display unit, working my way to the control tower, passing through its ever-changing batteries of data, weaving flight and weather information as on a great bright loom. . .

The boarding announcement came. When I rose and faced the tunnel, displaying my boarding pass to the attendant, there was a wavering, a darkening. I stared into a dank and shadowy cave, serpentine forms writhing upon its walls.

With my remaining objectivity, I estimated fifty paces to its turning, saw that there was no one before me, closed my eyes, extended my left hand to the side and counted them off, concentrating the while on the counting, the walking. . .

Fifty!

I opened my eyes then, saw that I was almost there and ran. I took the turn, passed into a larger, longer version of the death-wagon, and begged a steward to show me to my seat.

"Forgot my glasses," I whined. "Can't read the numbers. . ."

He was sympathetic, even if he did develop a third eye, orange skin and green hair on the way back to 13A, a window seat.

I strapped in, kicked my bag under the seat before

me and huddled, trembling. The murmuring voices
all about me seemed part of a sinister conspiracy,
directed toward myself. I cursed, I prayed, and finally I coiled again, remaining a part of the plane's
systems until we were airborne.

But distractions would come. It was a long flight.

I heard the steward ask me whether I wanted a
drink. I told him to bring me a double Scotch and
passed him the money, intentionally not looking at
him. In doing so, however, I glanced toward the
window.

There was no window. It was all open air, as I had
somehow known it would be. Stormclouds boiled
beneath us. We were riding in a long, wide, open
cart, and before us, tossing their curled horns and
blowing fire, a thunder-black team of demonic
horses dragged us toward a distant moun-
tainpeak—Brocken, I knew—where fires flashed
and a giant shadow swayed in the sky, tiny figures
dancing below it. . .

And my fellow passengers—ugly, malevolent,
bats darting about them, black cats in their laps, a
prevalence of handmade brooms. We were headed
for a witches' sabbath, and of course I knew who was
to be the sacrifice. . .

My drink arrived—a sickly yellow-green in color,
with drops of an oily substance floating on its surface.

I took it and closed my eyes. I sniffed it. It was
Scotch. I took a large swallow and coughed. It was
Scotch.

It warmed my belly like an explosion. I kept my
eyes closed. I told myself that I was aboard an
airplane headed for Philadelphia. I reached out and

touched the cold glass of the window. I felt the back of the seat before me. Silently, I recited what I could remember of the Gettysburg Address. I listened to the flight computer for a time. I thought of Cora. . .

Yes, Cora. I'm coming. They're not going to stop me that easily—just a few demons, ghouls, assorted monsters. I know I'm making them up just to keep the trip interesting, to square my mental and emotional accounts. I'm not going crazy. The next time you see me, I'll be eminently rational as a result. I look upon all of this as cathartic, a beneficial working-out of everything that's been bothering me at the most basic levels. I'm not going crazy. Honestly, Cora, I can't be going crazy at this point, can I? It would be the ultimate in irony to gain so much—you, my own identity—and then to blow it all by going off the deep end. No, I have to believe that all of this is serving a higher end— rationality. It must, it must. . .

I took another drink. Better. A little bit better now. Whatever was there hadn't hurt me so far. And wasn't the coven relaxing with drinks of its own now, anyway? Sigh, BelPatri. When did you give up smoking? It seems that you used to. . .

And then the hand was tipped, and I knew that I had been had.

"Would you care for a snack, sir?"

Automatically, I opened my eyes as I replied in the negative. The steward was still monstrous, but my gaze went past him, out, down, into the open temple of columns, blocks, statuary above which we were passing, where youths played flutes and maidens danced. And there, in its midst, upon a kind of altar between flaming braziers, two gray old women were

dismembering a child with their bare hands, tearing
at it, crushing the bones in their jaws, blood stream-
ing from their mouths. They became aware of my
gaze. They turned and shook their fists.

It was horrible, yet it was also familiar. It was—
" 'Snow'," I said aloud. " 'Snow'! God damn you! I
remember!"

It was Hans Castorp's dream in the chapter titled
"Snow" in Thomas Mann's *The Magic Mountain*—
which I had read in a Lit. course back in college,
which I had mentioned to Ann, discovering that she,
too, had read the book. We had spent an entire evening discussing the significance of that scene, of the
merging of the Apollonian and Dionysiac, the Clas-
sical and the formless, intellect and emotion—

She knew what an impression it had made upon
me once.

I took a deep breath. I smelled lilies of the valley.
The aroma had been with me all along, subliminal,
overwhelmed by the sensory assaults.

My dear Ann, I said silently, if you are capable of
hearing what I am thinking right now—screw you!
You slipped up on that one. I know what you're
doing. I know where you're coming from. It's not
good enough.

The view below me wavered, grew insubstantial. I
was sitting in an airplane, with normal people. I was
not going crazy, my psyche was not turning itself
inside-out. She was somehow projecting hallucinations at me. But that was all that they were—all
shadow and no substance.

Minutes later, they returned. We were being attacked by super-fast pterodactyls which tore pieces
out of the wings. I regarded them coldly for a time

and then closed my eyes again. They were still distracting, and I wanted to think about important matters, like what I was going to say to my former employers when I reached their headquarters.

SIX

. . . And came down, as the man said.

The sea-green Ouroboros serpent which had wrapped itself around the plane faded as we entered the landing pattern. We swept in, touched down perfectly and taxied to our gate with no delays.

As I emerged from the tunnel, this one uncluttered with horrors, an airline agent—a short, dark-haired stock character in a crisp uniform—approached me.

"Mr. BelPatri?"

"Yes."

"*Donald* BelPatri?"

"Right."

"Would you come this way, please?"

I took a couple of steps with him, out of the traffic. Then, "Where are you taking me?" I asked.

"The VIP lounge, sir."

"Now why would you want to do that?"

"There is a gentleman there, waiting to see you."

"And who might that be?"

"I don't know his name, sir."

"Well . . ." I said. "Let's go and find out."

I walked with him for a time. We finally turned up a short corridor. He opened the door and showed me in.

There were four people in the lounge, three men and a woman. Two of the men were flunkies, I could see that right away—large, young and athletic-looking, with open-necked shirts under light jackets; clean-cut; bodyguard types. They were standing behind the older, jovial-seeming, white-haired man who sat at a table, facing me. He wore a dark, well-tailored jacket, white shirt, somber necktie. There was a bottle of mineral water on the table, and the three of them held glasses of clear, sparkling liquid. Not so the woman. She held a big, wicked-looking drink in an old-fashioned glass. She was seated at the man's right. Arresting features and complexion—quadroon, I'd say—with very bleached hair. Somewhere around forty. Had on a pretty yellow blouse with ruffles, a strand of dark beads about her neck. Stouter now than I remembered her, I saw, as she rose along with the man, to greet me. Her name was Marie—Marie Melstrand—I knew, as suddenly as I could recall having known her before. I couldn't remember much else about her, though. Both of them smiled at me.

"Don, how is everything?" The Boss inquired.

The Boss . . . We almost always called him just that. His name, however, was Creighton Barbeau, chairman of the board of Angra Energy.

We . . . ? I wasn't certain exactly who all the pronoun covered, as I possessed only a partial memory here. But there were images of myself as a member of some sort of group of special people who worked for him. And Marie, Marie was one of us.

"Everything is very interesting lately," I said. "How'd you know I was on that plane?"

He squinted his left eye and smiled, which I knew meant that he considered that a foolish question. Of course, I ought to know that he knew everything. . .

"I'm concerned about you, Don," he said, moving around the table, coming up to me, squeezing my shoulder. "You don't look real well. I thought we were taking better care of you. Getting tired of Florida?"

"I'm getting tired of a lot of things," I said.

"Surely," he agreed, taking my arm. "Completely understandable. Not everybody likes an early retirement." Automatically, I let him guide me to the table. "Care for a drink?"

"Not now, thanks."

". . . But you know how it was," he went on, raising his glass for a sip. "A lot of trouble there, getting you out of the way in time."

He set it down and gave me a full, direct, open-seeming gaze.

"Not that you weren't worth it, of course, God knows. But things were a bit ticklish for awhile. Couldn't take any chances. Always worth going out of your way for a good man, though."

"Donald," Marie said, in her precise way, before I could get off a reply. She extended her hand and I took it, again automatically.

"Marie," I said. "How've you been?"

"Not hurting," she answered, "and getting better

at what I do. What more can a person ask?"

"Indeed," I said, feeling something a trifle hostile behind her smiling mask.

"I've thought of you a lot, Don," The Boss was going on. "You've been missed, you know. Considerably."

"Where's Cora?" I said, turning toward him.

"Cora?" He furrowed his brows. "Oh, Cora. Of course. Someone did mention her to me—a lady you've been seeing recently. You know—you know, Don—I'd be willing to bet that she never left the state at all. I'll bet she's still down in the Keys, looking for you right now. Had a little pout and left, changed her mind. You should really have left her a message."

I felt slightly uncomfortable at that, because of the bare possibility that there might be some truth in it. He pressed on then, before I could voice any doubts:

"You know, I don't think you really came here looking for her," he said, conspiratorially. "Maybe that's what you told yourself, but I think it was something different. I think maybe you're feeling better now than you were a few years ago. I think you came up here, whether you realize it or not, looking for some action. I think you really want your old job back."

He studied my features at this last—almost hopefully, I'd say.

"I don't remember my old job all that well," I answered him. "*Is* Cora here?"

"We could use you, if you're up to it again," he continued quickly. "Of course you could expect a sizable raise. Hate to see my people suffering from inflation. The competition's getting pretty fierce, you know? That big lead we had in solar energy's just been melting away. Too damn much government interference—and the other guys have been spying on us like something out of James Bond. Got to hand it to them, though. They've come up with some clever tricks for that sort of thing—and it's costing plenty just to keep them at arms' distance. Not that they could ever hold a candle to one of my top people, if you catch my meaning. Bet you could really throw them the shaft."

"Look," I said. "Maybe so and maybe not. But it's Cora I want to hear about right now. *Do* you know where she is?"

"Don, Don, Don . . ." he sighed. "You don't seem to understand what I'm saying. We really can use you again. I'm offering you your old job back on even better terms. We want you to rejoin the family. People look at me sometimes when I talk that way, but I really do think of all my personal aides as a family. I can't think of anything I wouldn't do for them to make their lives a little brighter."

"Cora," I said through clenched teeth.

"Might even help you look for your lady friend," he said then.

"You're saying you *don't* know where she is?"

"Don't know," he said. "We'll help you, though, if you'll help us."

"I think you're lying."

"Now that hurts, Don," he answered. "I try to be square with my people."

"Okay," I said. "I know you keep records on everything—clandestine as well as above-board. Let me look, if that's the case. Let me check the Double Z files on current quiet stuff."

"And you said your memory was bad. But that's right, you did work in Double Z a lot. Guess that would be hard to forget. All right. It grieves me that you don't trust my word, but if you want to check the records, you can. Anything you want. We can go and look at them right now."

Was that a mocking light in Marie's eyes as she raised her glass and drained it?

The Boss made a motion to his Muscle. They crossed the room. One of them opened a door—not the one I had come in by.

He held it open. The other passed outside. Marie picked up her purse from the floor and got to her feet. She and Barbeau began moving toward the doorway. I followed them.

We exited, to come upon a small, private parking lot. The bodyguard who had preceded us was already climbing into a limousine. There was something more than a little suspicious to me about the ease with which The Boss had agreed to give me a ride over to the shop for an inspection of secret records.

The limousine came to life. It moved.

"This is very cooperative of you," I said, "but I'm not really prepared to inspect them immediately. I want my lawyer on hand when I do."

I didn't really have a lawyer in the area, but if I called Ralph Dutton I'd a feeling he could put me in touch with someone competent.

"A lawyer?" he said, turning toward me as the car swung around. "Come on, Don! This is just between us. I don't want some legal eagle sniffing around while you're pulling out sensitive stuff."

"I'll come by in the morning, to the front door," I

said, "with counsel. I want to have lots of explanations then—like what I was supposed to have done that got me sent out to pasture with my brains washed. I'll want to talk about that, too."

The car pulled up before us, halted.

The big man at his side moved forward and opened doors. I took a step backward and let my hands hang loose. I adjusted my balance. I'd a feeling that the bodyguard was going to try forcing me into the car. If so—

"Well, if that's the way you feel about it," Barbeau said, "I'm sorry. I'm really sorry that we can't just work this out between us, like in the old days." He turned one palm upward. "But, if that's the way it has to be, okay. Bring your man around in the morning and we'll do it your way."

He and Marie climbed into the back seat.

"Good-bye, Donald."

The bodyguard shut them in, got into the front passenger seat and closed the door. I watched them drive off.

Hell of an anticlimax. It was absolutely too easy. Unless—

Could it be possible that I had really misread the situation? I had had amnesia. Supposing everything I'd seen on the way up had been bona fide BelPatri hallucinations? Could I really rely on my own judgment? What if Cora *had* simply gotten tired of putting up with me and left? Maybe—

I turned away. That way lies . . . I chuckled. More madness? Come on, feet, take me away. I looked around the area. The only pedestrian exit from the parking lot was a nearby platform—a station on the automated monorail system used to move people

around the airport. I crossed over and climbed its
steps.

I saw the button on the post, and there was an
instruction plate beneath it. This was a special station. Cars would not stop here unless someone coming out of the VIP lot signalled for one. The idea
apparently was that curious or wandering members
of the general public would not be able to get off at
this place. I pushed the button.

A few seconds later, a single car came along. There
was one man in it. He was sitting with his back to
me. I entered.

For a moment, I stared. There was something
familiar about that seated figure. I moved around,
nearer to him, and I looked him in the face.

A gray man, in some indeterminate region of middle age. He had grown bushy sideburns and acquired a network of broken veins across his wide
nose since last I had seen him. He was a bit fleshier
now, with the pouches under his bright blue eyes
more pronounced.

"Willy Boy," I said.

No, the face on the houseboat in Florida had not
been his. It was as if my memory and imagination
had somehow combined to warn me about something even then.

"Well, bless me! If it isn't Mr. Don Bell-Patri!" he
said, in that magical voice, clear and almost musical.

That voice had once been nationally famous. The
words were always clearly enunciated; the accent
varied, seeming at different times to come from all
parts of the South. He'd shouted the Gospel at tent
audiences and then auditorium audiences and fi-

nally at millions watching him on television. There were healings and hollerings, and then there had been the story of the teen-age girl in Mississippi— her abortion, her attempted suicide . . . Willy Boy's stock had plummeted. In the end, there had been no legal charges, but for the past several years the faithful had been denied his version of the Lord. Willy Boy's profile had flattened on the graph of public awareness. But there was still something special about him. It involved the healings. They had been real.

"Matthews," I acknowledged, and I dropped into a seat facing him, fascinated by his presence, new memories surfacing from moment to moment.

I was fascinated, too, by the change that I saw in him—a change for the worse. He seemed to exhale evil now, along with a faint aroma of bourbon. And in a way, I was glad of this, because it meant that I had not been wrong, that I was not crazy, and that what was happening was not yet over.

The monorail car was not moving. Its door still stood wide open. But for the moment I thought nothing of this.

"How's the energy business these days?" I asked him—because he was part of the group, I felt sure of that much, though what the group was was still hazy to me. I wondered what Matthews did—

And then I remembered what he did, even as he began to do it to me. I felt a sudden shortness of breath, and then a pain in my chest and one that radiated down my left arm.

There had been a night, long ago, when I had gone with Willy Boy to his apartment and spent an evening lowering the level in a jug of very smooth white lightning. Incongruously, for what he did in those days, there was still an opened Bible in plain sight, on a small table by the window. Curious, when he was out of the room, I had gone over. It was opened to Psalm 109, which was almost entirely underlined. Later, when we were both several sheets to the wind, I had asked him about his preaching days:

"How much of it was hype? Did you really believe any of the things you said?"

He lowered his glass and raised his eyes. He fixed me with that acetylene blueness which had come over so well on the tube.

"I believed," he said simply. "So help me, when I started I was full of the fire of the Lord. I wanted their souls for Him. I believed. I hollered and gave 'em Scripture and waved the Good Book. I was as good as Billy Graham, Rex Humbard—any of 'em! Better, even! When I prayed for healing and saw 'em throw down their crutches and walk, or see again, or stop hurting, I knew that the grace of the Lord was on me, and I believed and there was no hype." His eyes drifted away from me. "Then one day I got mad at a newsman," he went on, slowly. "I kept telling him to move back, he was getting in my way. He wouldn't do it. 'Damn you, then!' I thought. 'Drop dead, you miserable bastard!' " He paused again. "And he did," he finally said. "just keeled over and lay there. The doctor said it was a heart attack. But he was young and healthy-looking, and I knew what I'd said in my heart. And then I thought about it. Thought about it a lot. Now the Lord wouldn't go in for His servant pulling that sort of thing, would He? The healing, yeah—if it was helping to get a bunch of 'em saved. But killing 'em? I started thinking, maybe the power didn't come from the Lord, maybe it was just something I could do by myself, either way. Maybe He didn't care one way or the other whether I was preaching or not preaching. It wasn't the Holy Spirit moving through me, healing. It was just something about me that could cure 'em or kill 'em. I started drinking around then, and fornicating and all the rest. That's when it got to be hype and makeup and TV cameras and people planted in the audience with fake testimonies . . . I didn't believe anymore. There's just us and animals and plants and rocks. There ain't no more. The best thing a man can do is get hold of all the good things in a hurry, 'cause time's passing fast. There's no God. Or if there is, He don't like me anymore.''

He took a big swallow then, refilled his glass and changed the subject. It was a part of the longest conversation I'd ever had with Willy Boy on anything other than business.

. . . And his business was killing people. Heart attack, cerebral hemorrhage—it always looked like natural causes. He had the power. He was a reverse faith healer with no faith. I think he hated himself and he took it out on other people, for money, for Angra. And now he was squeezing my heart, and I would be dead in a matter of seconds.

I started to get up. I fell back. He was not finishing me as quickly as he might have. This was something new—overt sadism. He wanted to watch me struggle and die slowly.

I rolled out of my seat to the floor. A sense of the train's computerized guidance system was in my brain like an alarm. Without knowing how I was doing it, I was trying to get the car to move, to take me to where I could get help. I reached the door, which had closed a few moments before, and I couldn't get it open again. I pushed and pulled at it with my right hand, my left arm now feeling as if it were afire. Through the glass, I now became aware of a vague shape outside—a large man—a third bodyguard, perhaps. He just stood there watching while I struggled.

Matthews' whiskered face loomed over me as he leaned forward in his seat, showing his long yellowed teeth, engulfing me in an atmosphere of alcohol fumes. I tried to reach out with all of my strength. Something—

The car suddenly lurched under me, back and forth, back and forth, a rapid, violent shaking. Willy Boy was jostled out of his seat.

The pressure in my chest eased. Abruptly, the door opened.

I half-crawled, half-rolled out of the car onto the platform and began to scramble away. The only safety from Matthews' attacks, I remembered, lay in distance. If I could get more than a stone's throw away from Willy Boy, he couldn't kill me, not with his mind alone.

I practically threw myself to my feet. I swayed, recovered and took a step, halted again, as a wave of dizziness came and went. The man who had been waiting on the platform still had a look of surprise on his face. Old Willy Boy wasn't supposed to let them get away. Behind me, I could still hear the car lurching back and forth, as the man recovered and came at me.

He aimed a kick, and my body responded before my memory did. I had some skill here that I had not recalled.

My arm, fist clenched, moved in a scooping block that caught his leg and broke his balance, sending him toppling backward, rolling to the side and right off the edge of the platform. He fell onto the track, where a single large rail stood up from a narrow roadbed.

Turning, I saw Matthews being shaken from his feet within the lurching car. Booze and age had slowed his reflexes. As he struggled to rise once more he was toppled again, but this time nearer to the doors. Now he tried crawling. He was almost to them. He was partway through. . .

With a vicious crash the doors slammed shut on him. Their edges were padded, but they had closed hard and they remained closed, clamping him in place.

Immediately then, the car ceased its shaking. It accelerated rapidly and I heard a scream from below, where the other man had fallen. I did not look down. It had been a very final thing—the unmistakable crunching sound of the car's impact upon a body, the abrupt termination of the scream, a certain smell. . .

And back, back off to my left now as I turned, I could still see Matthews' head protruding from between the doors of the receding car, his face dark and contorted, his mouth working but no words coming out.

A moment of nausea came and went. I looked all around me. The monorail's roadbed seemed the handiest route for flight. I jumped down upon it, far past the thing that lay unmoving beside the track, my eyes averted. Then I turned and began running in the direction opposite that which the car had taken.

Something had helped me, I knew that. What or
how, though, I had no time to speculate. I wanted to
put as much distance as I could between myself and
that platform in the shortest time possible. I ran, my
breath coming hard into my lungs, my heart pounding.

This went on for what could have been several
minutes. I don't know. Then I felt the ground vibrating beneath my feet. My first thought was that a big
plane was taking off or landing somewhere nearby,
masked by the surrounding structures. But it grew
stronger and acquired an above-ground accompani-
ment that I couldn't mistake. Another monorail car
was coming toward me.

A moment later it came into view, rounding a
corner up ahead. Inside, I could see the passengers,
pulling emergency switches or cords to which the
vehicle was not apparently responding. None of
them were yet looking in my direction.

I was about to leap from the track to get out of the
way when the car suddenly began braking. There
was no platform in sight, but it came to a halt and
the door opened. I ran forward and climbed in.

The doors snapped shut behind me and the car
jerked into motion again, this time heading back in
the direction from which it had come.

I grabbed hold of one of the hanging loops and
stood panting. Everyone in the car turned to stare at
me. I felt a crazy, light-headed desire to laugh.

"Just a test run," I muttered. "Getting ready for
the Pope's visit."

They continued to stare, but shortly a platform
came into sight, thronged with people. The car
halted there in good order and the doors opened.

I stepped out and passed among the others, running a hand through my hair, adjusting my apparel, brushing away dust, before I gave way to tremblings. I had a strong desire then to fling myself onto a nearby bench. But a death-trap had just been sprung, wheel turning upon wheel, rods dancing, delicate balances shifting, all to crush me; and someone or something had reached out and realigned a gear-setting, jogged a balance, reset the final closure in my favor, burying all discomfort beneath the triumph of survival. It would be discourteous to ruin all that by collapsing now.

I kept going.

SEVEN

I got into the first of a line of cabs waiting outside the terminal, and I told the driver to take me into town. I half-expected to hear sirens at any moment, and I sat tensely much of the way in, staring out of the window, at other cars, at trees, at buildings, at signs along the road. The sun was working its way into the west, but there was still plenty of daylight remaining. I had to get out of town, had to put a lot of distance between me and this part of the country in a hurry, had to find a place to hole up, think this thing through, formulate a plan. Couldn't think now, though; something could happen at any minute. Had to keep my wits handy. I was certain that this cab ride would eventually be traced, which was why I was heading into town. I hoped to confuse the trail.

I had her drop me on a busy, random, downtown corner. I walked until I came to a bus stop. I stood there watching people and pigeons. I got into the first bus that came along and rode it for a long while in a roughly northwesterly direction. When it took a turn to the south I got off at the next stop and began walking again, to the north and the west.

I rode two more buses and walked a lot before I reached a suburban area. Then I tried sticking out my thumb to passing motorists. I had a feeling of having done it before, years earlier, back when I was in school. Yes, I'd wanted to go home for the semester break my first year, and I didn't want to spend the money. I remembered that it had gotten pretty cold and windy between rides. Smile a little. That sometimes seems to help. . .

. . . A number of required general courses and my Computer Science major requirement. I'd done pretty well. It had been a bit lonely at first, but I'd a few friends now—like Sammy, who used to call me "Mumbles"—and I was anxious to get home and talk about everything. Mumbles? I hadn't thought of that nickname in years. Sammy was in my Comp. Sci. section, a little dark-eyed guy with a warped sense of humor. I'd had a habit of muttering when I was working with computers. Actually, I used to talk to them—give them names and all. He never knew that. He just heard me at it and started calling me Mumbles. We became pretty good friends as time went on. I wondered where he was now? Be nice to call him someday and see whether he remembers me. . .

Actually, I hadn't started talking to the machines in college. It went back to my parents' business when I was much younger. I used to play games with the computers. I started talking to them then, I guess. Outside of that one experience when I was about seven, though, I hadn't gotten much in the way of personal responses from them. But I'd always had a feeling that if I tried hard enough—

A car slowed down. An older man in a lightweight business suit pulled over.

"How far you going?" he asked.

"Pittsburgh, actually," I said.

"Well, I'm just going home to Norristown," he said, "but I can drop you at the Turnpike, if you like."

"Great."

I got in.

He didn't seem to be looking for conversation, so I leaned back and tried to continue my reverie. It had been broken, though, and nothing new seemed willing to surface. All right. I no longer felt as harried as I had in the cab. Maybe I could think a little more clearly now about my present situation. Then I might be able to initiate some action of my own instead of merely running, reacting.

Barbeau was definitely out to kill me now. No doubt about that. And Matthews was still working for him, as was the rest of the group. . .

The group. . . It was somehow the key. It had once included me, as much as I hated to think of it now. It also included Willy Boy, and Marie Melstrand. Cora? No, she'd never been involved. I really had met her for the first time on her Florida vacation. And Ann Strong? Very much so. There had been the four of us. Yes. Four of us with something in common. . .

We all had odd mental powers. I talked with machines, I possessed a form of human-to-computer telepathy. I could read their programs at a distance. Marie? Marie's power was a force she could exert upon *things*. PK, they used to call it. While she could wreck a computer, she was incapable of reading it the way I could. Ann? Ann was a human-to-human telepath. She couldn't read computers either, but she could both receive and transmit information, from and to other people—up to and including real-seeming visual impressions. And Willy Boy . . . ? A kind of PK, I suppose, but not quite. His was a subtle form of physiological manipulation, working with matter and energy inside living systems exclusively.

How good were they? What were their limits? Another memory came through . . . Marie took great pride in her cooking, and she *was* good. I recalled that she'd had us all over for dinner on several occasions. Rather than fool with padded gloves or pot-holders, she had once, while seated at the table, levitated a huge tureen of steaming soup out in the kitchen, causing it to drift eerily into the dining room and settle to a perfect landing before us. I'd seen her spill a drink and freeze the droplets in midair, then cause them all to drift back into the glass without moistening anything nearby. The maximum mass she could affect . . . ? Once, on a bet, she had raised Ann several feet above the floor and held her there for half a minute, but she was panting and sweating before the time was up, and she let her down kind of hard. . .

Old Willy Boy . . . The nearer you were to him the faster he could affect you. Sudden death within ten feet, a little slower out to twenty—thirty or forty feet caused him a lot more work, slowed him considerably. I'd say fifty feet was his absolute maximum, but that it might take him a quarter of an hour to get results at that range—strangely, the approximate radius of the larger tents he used to work in. Think-

ing about it, it occurred to me that I must now be one
of the few people to have felt both his healing and his
destroying touch. I recalled the morning after that
drinking session at his place. I had sacked out on the
sofa, and I awoke when I heard him moving around,
cursing. My head was splitting. I got up and walked
to his bathroom. He was in there gulping aspirins.
He grinned at me. "You don't look too good, boy,"
he'd said. I told him to save a couple for me. "What
for?" he answered, reaching out and tossling my
hair. "Heal! Heal, you sinner!" I'd felt a sudden rush
of blood to my head, my temples had throbbed for a
moment and then all of the pain was gone. I felt fine.
"I'm okay," I said, surprised at my undeserved recovery. "Praise the Lord!" he replied, taking a final
aspirin. "Why don't you do it for yourself?" I said
then. He'd shaken his head. "I can't work it on me.
My little cross in this vale of tears." And that was all
I knew about Willy Boy's power.

Ann . . . Her ability did not seem to fall off with
distance. She could have been sitting in a motel
room down in the Keys causing me to see that serpent as we were landing in Philadelphia. Her weaknesses were at some other level, and I couldn't recall
them. She did have a thing about flowers, though.
Reading their primitive life emanations somehow
soothed her. She returned to them whenever she was
troubled. They were so prominent in her mental life
that they often colored—or perfumed, I suppose—
her transmissions. And it seemed that she could also
make you *not* see something that was indeed present.

The four of us, then—a team, a set of tools for
Barbeau. We were the reason that Angra had outdis-
tanced all the competition some years ago. I could

steal data from anyone's computer. And if it wasn't there, Ann could pluck it from the minds that held it. Marie could ruin experiments, cause accidents, set back anyone's research project. And if some particular individual were really troublesome, a certain Southern gentleman might pass him on the street, sit near him in a theatre, eat at the same restaurant. . .

But could I be sure of the extent of everyone's abilities *now?* Back at the airport lounge, Marie had made a comment about getting better at what she did. Had everyone's powers continued to develop, to improve with the passage of time? An intangible. Impossible for me to estimate. Best to assume that they had. Give Matthews a few more feet, maybe, intensify Ann's hallucinations, assume Marie can lift a bit more, hold it a little longer. I never knew her range. Greater than Willy Boy's, nothing like Ann's. That was all.

What about Barbeau himself? Had he some special power beyond simple ruthlessness and a keen intellect? I didn't know. If he did, he either kept it well-hidden or I was missing that memory.

And where was Cora? What had they done with her? I doubted they would have harmed her. Dead, she would have been worthless to them as a hold over me. I hadn't seemed too tractable to Barbeau. Maybe there had been a signal from Ann to the effect that she had scanned me and that I was now useless to him. So he had not even bothered to offer a trade: Cora, for my coming back. On the other hand, he had known I was coming. He would take me back if I were willing, and he was ready to dispose of me if I were not. And just in case, just in case I got away, he wanted Cora for insurance. That seemed to make some kind of sense. I was certain that he had her alive, somewhere very safe.

The car began to slow. I peered ahead. It was getting on into evening now, and a bit harder to see . . . Traffic jam. An accident, maybe. I saw parked police cars.

No. It was a roadblock, near a little strip of parkland which filled the bulge between this and another highway. My stomach tightened. They were stopping everyone, letting them through slowly, one by one. Checking IDs, obviously.

Despite continuing civil libertarian protests, everyone had a Social Registration Card these days. They'd come in in the late '80s, providing one number for everything—Draft Registration, Social Security, Driver's License, voting, what have you. I could see now that, up ahead, the police were just looking at these cards and feeding the numbers through a little unit they carried.

I had known that an alarm would go out for me. But I had not expected anything this fast, this efficient. It was interesting, though, that they were after a number rather than a face. Perhaps Barbeau had not wanted just anyone to know which man he wanted so badly. Perhaps the police computer was merely set to identify my number. Perhaps it had been furnished mine and a list of phonies, so that they would not easily be able to ascertain my true identity. Yes, that seemed the way Barbeau would go about it.

I wondered, as we drew even nearer to the block—Should I simply tell the police my story, now that there were police available?

My more cynical self, which had been slow in making its comeback, sneered at the thought. At

best, they would take me to be confused, upset . . .
At worst—I did not know how many grains of truth
there had been in Barbeau's version of the past—
uncomfortably many, according to my own returning memory. Was I really guilty of some crime or
crimes of such scope that it had necessitated my
being retired with a new identity? Somehow, I did
not doubt that The Boss would have a better chance
of making charges stick against me than I would
against him.

My driver, who kept shaking his head, finally
pulled up to the roadblock in his turn.

"Let me see your ID, please. Your passenger's,
too," the nearest cop said.

He produced his own from an inside wallet, while
I fished for mine.

"What's the matter, officer?" he asked.

The policeman shook his head.

"Fugitive," he said.

"Dangerous?"

The cop looked at him and glanced at the second
car, upon the hood of which was perched an officer
holding a shotgun, and he smiled.

The driver passed him my SR card. Almost without thinking, I coiled into the small unit he wore
slung like an accordian and keyed with less musical
effect. It was one of the older units, I saw. With the
newer ones you could just push the card into a slot
for a direct read.

He punched my number, but a slightly different
signal went out. In the broadcast version a pair of
the digits had been transposed. An All Clear light
came on upon the face of the box. He handed back
the cards.

"Go on," he said, turning toward the next car.

We pulled away. The driver sighed. He had his headlights on now, as did the other vehicles.

It seemed only moments later that I heard a cry from behind us, followed by the shotgun's boom. A sound like hail came from all over the place.

"What the hell," the driver said, stepping on the gas rather than the brake.

But I had already begun to suspect. Someone, somewhere back at home base, must have been watching a printout or display screen. The machine cleared it, but to a human observer a pair of transposed digits still came awfully close to what they wanted. The possibility of operator error must have occurred to him and he had radioed out to have them halt us again. The fact that they were this trigger-happy made me wonder what they had been told and what their instructions must have been. I did not want to stay around to ask them personally. So. . .

"Stop!" I cried. "They'll shoot again!"

He finally hit the brake and we began to slow. I glanced back.

No time to wait for him to come to a complete stop. I needed every bit of the lead we had.

I opened the door and jumped out. I hit that grassy central strip, collapsed and rolled. I didn't look back as I recovered my feet. I ran for the woods, cutting to my left and then to my right as soon as I entered them. I heard gunshots far to the rear, but they had the sound of pistols.

The ground took an abrupt turn upward and I stumbled to mount it. The sounds of traffic came from above. I did not know what road it was, but it did not matter. I was heading for it now. It was dark, there were lots of trees between me and the police and the shouting had stopped. If I could just get out and get across the highway . . . It was almost too much to hope that I might be able to flag a ride. I was vaguely aware of blood on my hand and my face, and I was certain that my trousers were torn. . .

. . . They must have been told that I was armed and dangerous, maybe even a cop-killer, to come on shooting that way. I kept expecting to hear them behind me again at any moment. . .

Up ahead of me, pieces of the blackness moved, came together. Suddenly, they shot upward, towering, swaying, acquiring illumination as from strong moonlight. It was a bear! An enormous grizzly—I'd seen them in zoos—reared up on its hind legs, facing me! It—

Oh, no. Not again, Ann. Not here. Not that way. Not with a grizzly bear on the outskirts of Philadelphia. You should have tried a cop with a shotgun if you'd wanted to stop me. I'd have shit my pants and wouldn't have smelled your flowers. Better luck next time.

I headed straight toward it. I bit my lip and closed my eyes as I passed through, but I did pass through. When I opened them again I saw the lights of traffic through a final screen of trees. Not just a little traffic, though. It was heavy, a veritable river. There was no way I could get across it without being hit.

But I thought I heard voices in the woods below now. Not too damn much choice.

I burst out of the wooded strip onto the shoulder of the highway, waving my arms at everything in the nearest lane, wondering what sort of impression I made—bloody, dirty and ragged—there in their headlights.

. . . Smile a little. That sometimes seems to help. . .

I came to a halt and just kept waving. Definitely now, I could hear the sounds of my pursuers, working their way through the woods, yelling to each other. . .

A truck screeched to a halt before me. I could hardly believe it, but I was not about to question the driver's judgment. Behind it, an entire lane of vehicles was coming to a halt. I ran for it, pulled open the door and jumped in. I slammed it behind me and collapsed in the passenger seat. Immediately, the engine roared and we were moving. I felt like the Count of Monte Cristo, Willie Sutton and the Man Who Broke the Bank at Monte Carlo—lucky and free. For the moment, anyhow. At least, I wouldn't be shot for awhile and I was moving, away.

"Thanks," I said. "Maybe it looks funny, but I'll explain it as soon as I get my breath back. You're a real life-saver."

I breathed a couple of deep ones and waited. The engine had settled down to a steady, smooth purring. We were moving along at a very good clip, the countryside flashing by in a long, curving blur. I turned my head.

The driver's seat was as empty as a pawnbroker's heart.

I took a deep breath. There wasn't the faintest trace of daffodils, narcissi, lilies or any other plant's sexual organs, just the slightly stale, dusty smell of an area long enclosed.

I exhaled. What the hell.

"Thanks," I repeated, anyway.

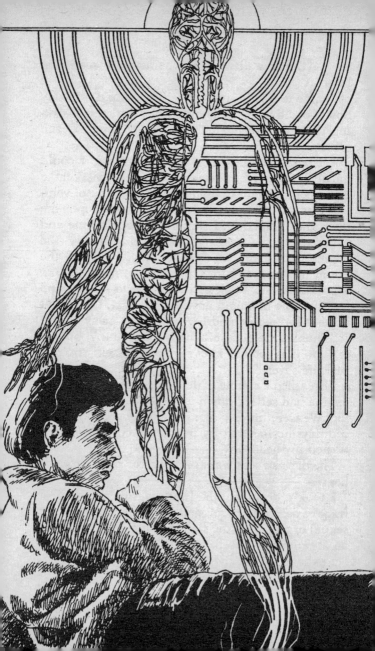

EIGHT

Speeding along through the dark tube of the night, towns and country rush together . . . The lights are bright beads, the sound of the engine soothing in its monotony. I had lapsed into a half-drowse in quick reaction to the day's events. . .

I was moving along at about one hundred-fifty kilometers an hour in one of the safest vehicles on the road. The truck was powered by large and expensive batteries, which were still economical because of the recent cheapness of electric power. A competing line of vehicles was fueled by hydrogen, clean and non-polluting, available now in unlimited supply again because of the cheap electricity produced by solar power. Both were largely the result of advances made under patents held by Angra Energy, with their vast new power installations producing electricity across the Sunbelt.

I remembered vividly how the substance of some

of the patents had been obtained. I was guilty of industrial espionage, though I wondered whether any statute really covered the specific methods I had used. Morally, though . . . Well . . . This was not a suitable time for soul-searching, though I wondered why it bothered me now when it hadn't then. Or had it? Or had I changed? Or both? There was a memory somewhere that I couldn't quite reach.

The truck I rode was completely automated, traveling only on specially equipped highways, though more and more roads were being fitted with the necessary equipment. Usually, they drove in one special lane. It was plainly marked, so that human drivers could avoid it if they wished. Actually, though, the automated trucks had proven safer than the traditional kind, and very few people objected to sharing the road with them.

All of this meant that I was safe, for the moment. But there were really a number of things I should be about. Only, it felt so good to be stretched out here on the right seat, which converted into a cot, my head propped slightly to see the lights in the sky as well as those along the way. The wind whistled about us, engines hummed below. Peripherally, I was aware of steady transfers of data, and this too was good. Every minute, I was getting farther and farther away from the scene of my troubles.

The cot was there, as well as some elementary plumbing, for the same reason that the truck was still fitted with a full set of manual controls and two seats. The Teamsters' Union had been given large blocks of stock in companies profiting from this accelerated trend to automation. They no longer raised serious objections to the gradual cutback in the number of drivers' jobs, but the issue of requiring a live driver on board was not completely dead. It had not exactly been a Big 10-4 all the way—more a forty-roger, finger-wave, 10-65. So, the trucks still came equipped and continuing negotiations still raised the possibility of some form of featherbedding. For which I was, at the moment, grateful. This because, in addition to the facilities, I had also located some freeze-dried food evidently left by the last human driver or passenger. I had eaten enough to take the edge off my hunger before I had collapsed the seat and stretched out, overcome by fatigue.

All right. I had to provide for my continuing safety. Which meant that I had to know as much as I could before I allowed myself the luxury of sleep. There was still too much that I did not know about this freight run and everything connected with my passage, and there was only one way that I could discover more—

Click. Clicket. Clicketderick.

Down, twisting, into, through, expanding now, out branches and sub-branches . . . Dots of light . . . Break-voids . . . The elegant symmetries of the programs and contingency programs within the onboard computer . . . Laid out like an incandescent formal garden . . . No scents here, however, and sense coded . . . Pause and consider its ways . . . The rest will come. . .

The computer steered and controlled speed, receiving information on road conditions and other matters through a communications strip buried in the pavement. Its radar probed continually on all sides for other traffic and for unexpected obstacles. In principle, it was similar to the manner in which the *Hash Clash* moved along the channels among the Keys, obtaining information from broadcast units on their banks. And at the same time as this one managed the driving, it was monitoring engine performance, the condition of the brakes and all other systems.

I passed in analogue through these various functions, coming to understand them as I did so. And this, in turn, provided a number of insights into the overall design. I coiled further then, attacking the travel-code. There were a number of obscurities— bits with no immediately apparent referents, the precise meanings of which would have to remain unknown until they were actually called into operation—but the general picture began to fall into place. It seemed likely that our destination was Memphis.

Further, further . . . Winding through the programs . . . The biggest question of all still pended . . . The Why still waved and fluttered like a bright banner before me . . . I ransacked the instructions until I came upon it—strange, and at the same time familiar. . .

Ricketerclick.

I withdrew from the bright microcosm, puzzled.

I groped beneath the dashboard then for a small first aid kit which the computer's inventory had told me should be present. I located it and brought it out. I found some bandages and an antibacterial ointment within.

There was also a small drum of water with a flexible hose and a tap nearby. I drank some and used some more to wash my cuts. I applied the ointment then and covered the wounds.

Running in darkness like a company of migrating creatures, untouched and untouching, the great trucks bent their course across the land. We maintained a precise distance from the one before us. If a car cut in there was an immediate adjustment. The lane in harmony lay to the central beat of the mechanical heart. I felt the stern march of its program all about me. Yet—

I had seen it there . . . My signature. As plain as if it were in longhand. I had seen it as I had seen that it was the hand of a stranger rather than Cora's which had left the message back at my condo. It made no sense . . . And yet it made sense.

I reclined myself completely, to where only gangs of passing stars were visible beyond the window. More thinking was definitely in order, and I stoked my tired brain and sought the tracks of reason.

The instruction that the truck stop back when it did to pick me up had not been a part of its original programming package. I had seen the alterations in its instructions, and it had been plain to me that I had somehow put them there myself. I had ordered the truck to stop for me. But how? I had never done anything like that before, had never been able to, was not even certain how to go about it.

And then I was uncertain of my uncertainty. There was the matter of the transposed digits when the policeman had punched out my SR number. Had he really made a mistake, or had an alteration occurred in the signal itself? I wondered. Was my signature on that one, too?

And the odd behavior of the monorail cars back at the terminal . . . I had been striving to do—something—as Willy Boy applied his cardiac arrest routine. Even then, could I have been operating at some new level?

I again recalled Marie's words—". . . getting better at what I do". Had my ability continued to develop, along new lines, during its long period of quiescence? Had all of the recent stresses to which I had been subjected then forced me to use it in this new range, my much-abused subconscious pulling the strings?

If this were the case, and if I could learn to do it consciously, I saw a travel insurance policy suddenly presented.

But I continued to rack my still-incomplete memory. Nothing. I had always been a passive receiver, monitoring the internal activity of data processing equipment. I could not recall a single earlier instance where I had ever actually altered the programming. Now, it seemed that it could not have come to pass at a more appropriate time.

Terdickterclick.

. . . And around and in, again. The magical landscape lay all about me. I sought the place my mind chose to perceive as a fiery waterfall dropping into a bright yellow pool . . . Yes. There.

I plunged into the pool.

Down, down . . . Down through the immaterial linkages with the communications strip beneath the pavement . . . Now, like an underground river, flung . . . Rushing, off and away, into the vast, interconnected network of terminals and processors and junctions . . . What I had in mind would require adjustments at both ends. . .

Now, could I affect the pattern of the flow?

I willed it. I pushed. Spread out myself, both here and there, I strove to alter things at both the broadcast and reception ends, to change the characteristic signal which continuously reported the vehicle's position to the central traffic control systems. On the far end, I worked to alter the record, to make it suitable and proper. . .

I watched the bits fly by, like a line of blazing bees. . .

Success.

I had disguised the vehicle I was riding in. When Barbeau discovered that I had not been hit and killed trying to run across the highway and that I could not be located on the other side either, he would begin to wonder who or what might have stopped at night to pick up a bleeding refugee. Let him wonder. Let him look. This truck had not passed that way.

I trickled through systems for the sheer pleasure of the ride, resisting the temptation to tamper in small ways for the fun of it. A feeling of enormous elation passed through me at the realization of this new aspect of my power. If Barbeau only knew what I had now, what mightn't he offer me?

Cora? And my life?

No. I did not want to work for him again. I would find another way. But first. . .

I lost control for a moment. My mind was filled with weather maps . . . I was lying in a field being rained upon, watching the advance of a high pressure front. It looked like a huge H in the sky . . . Miles away, I realized that my real body was yawning . . . I . . . I was falling asleep . . . My mind was drifting . . . I had done what I had set out to do . . . and now it was time to go back . . . but it was so pleasant just to drift into and out of the data-bases, floating on the systems streams, stroked by the pulses . . . washed by the baseball scores . . . I was. . .

I slept. Never before had I dreamed in the coils of

the data-net, never before had I surrendered my consciousness in such a state. But the fatigue had caught up with me—and I was gone—before I knew it. . .

Asleep in the arms of the data-sea, asleep in the coils of the deep. . .

I dreamed. I dreamed as I had never dreamt before, and only fragments protruded above the skyline of wakefulness, later. . .

I dreamed that I was a computer—a vast, ultrasophisticated one—existing in a kind of Limbo. A shadowy figure came and stood before me. While I did not exactly know this individual, it was not unfamiliar.

It moved to a keyboard and punched out a query—I do not remember what—requiring that I search my data-banks.

Whatever it was that it wanted involved an extraordinary amount of information. My printer hummed and the copy began to emerge.

The dark figure took the printout pages into its hands without tearing them loose and began to scan them at a rate which equalled my rate of output. They passed in a steady, shuffling cataract into accordian-pleated heaps upon the floor. Gradually the figure, still reading, was immersed within them.

When I ended my response the papers were swept away as by a sudden gust of wind, and the figure keyed another question. Again I responded. And again. And again.

Finally, it was typing upon my keyboard—something long and involved which did not really require a response on my part. It was trying to program in—well, tell me something. This input went on and on and on, and I was not really understanding all of it. Frustrated, the figure tried several more times. . .

All that I remembered, from the crazy games the waking consciousness plays with dream materials, was, NET LOT TO THE MARRIAGE OF TRUE MINDS, IMPEDIMENTS REMIT. . .

Amazing, the order in which a recovering memory recovers, the images in which we clothe things, the commonplaces within the mysterious, and vice-versa.

I awoke back inside my own skull and feeling somewhat rested. There was a moment of disorientation, and then the entire previous day's doings returned to me. I sat up and looked out of the window. Countryside, with a pre-dawn paling of the sky off to my left. . .

I took a drink of the flat-tasting water, my throat feeling rather dry, then used the sanitary facility. I washed and combed and sponged a few spots from my clothing. Then I opened some nourishing but otherwise undistinguished rations and broke my fast while staring ahead and trying to remember something that seemed very important.

Something had happened. What, I was not certain. I did not doubt that I had actually altered the truck's signal and its reception. But there was something more. While not on a level with Hans Castorp's, perhaps, I felt that my dream did hold some significance. Maybe I was really a computer dreaming I was a man.

The truck gave a sudden lurch, and I looked up in

time to see a girl in bluejeans, a heavy sweater and
tennis shoes pass out of sight to the left. What the
devil was she doing in the middle of the highway?
Then, up ahead, the figure of a young man crossed
before me—not too quickly, and not at all like a
person running for his life. His movements were
studied—with almost a dance-like quality to them.
The radar, of course, picked him up immediately
and my truck slowed. Then he was left behind, in the
interlane area on my left, passing as the similarly
garbed girl had passed.

Shortly, we braked again. There was no one before
me, but naturally my truck would brake if the one
before it braked, and it of course would brake if the
one before it braked, and so on down the line.

Another jerk, and we were going more slowly.
Another—

We passed two more of the youths, who had obviously repeated their predecessors' performances
here farther along the line.

And then I recalled having seen or read something
concerning the practice. They were referred to vari-
ously as truck-bashers, truck-dancers and truck-
dumpers. They got their kicks—usually in the early
morning or late at night, when there were few wit-
nesses passing in the "live" lanes—by dancing into
and out of the automated lanes on the big highways.
Knowing that the vehicles' radars would detect
them and that their computers were programmed to
keep them from striking foreign objects, they were
aware of their own relative safety. Some merely
enjoyed causing alterations in the speed and flow of
the long lines of automated vehicles. Others had
somewhat more catastrophic aims, in that their objective was to so alter the trucks' speed in a short

period of time as to overload the control systems and cause a long chain of accidents to occur. Of course, there was *some* danger to this—outside of one's possibly passing into the "live" lane while it was active—for they were gambling on the skill of the very same robot drivers whose systems they were attempting to overload.

Was it just kids indulging in the newest way of getting kicks? I wondered. Or was it yet another incarnation of Luddism—that old imperative to smash the evil machines which are wrecking life as we know it—now transferred from sinister engines to the computerized, the automated?

Or might it be neither of these, but something running deeper still and possibly a thing slightly more encouraging? I was reminded of something one of my professors had once said about ritual games and festal contests as being a general part of the human condition. Could the behavior I had witnessed represent a sort of modern rite of passage into the age of automation, an affirmation on the part of youth that man is still superior to his creations?

We lurched again. Damn kids! Irresponsible foolery is what it was. Too much time on their hands. They ought to. . .

. . . be out stealing industrial secrets?

Well, maybe I'd done a few socially unacceptable things myself when I was a bit younger. Of course, there had been reasons—if I could only recall them.

The ride smoothed out and we picked up speed again. Ritual ended, whatever. And the thing I had been trying to remember danced tantalizingly nearer.

The day continued to brighten. Haystacks and

farmhouses emerged from the night's retreating
tide.

And then the image of the dancer recurred within
my mind, flagrant passer in the dawnlight, arms
waving through radar pulses, feet measuring some
secret beat. To prove one's self superior to the
juggernaut by passing the body before it? To redirect the motions of the monster? To—

Redirect?

Change?

Alter?

Control?

The new, improved version of the power . . . I
wondered. It should be possible for me to work my
way back from here—terminal by terminal, connection by connection, through the data-net—coming
at last to Big Mac, the computer banks at Angra
Energy. The installation was hedged about with
every conceivable security defense, to protect Angra
from others doing what we had done unto them.
There were codes and scramblers, a security kernel
. . . Phrases such as "hierarchical design", "step-
wise refinement" and "Parnas modularity" passed
through my mind, recalled from the days when I had
worked to set up some of Big Mac's protections. Of
course, everything must have been overhauled, re-
vised, refined, pushed to much higher levels of
sophistication in the intervening years. But, on the
other hand, it seemed that something similar might
have happened to me. If I could penetrate Big Mac
and reach the Double Z sector, I was certain that
information concerning Cora would lie within. My
rite of passage, perhaps, to the new state toward
which I had been growing—if I could manage it. . .

All of these thoughts passed through my mind in a matter of moments, and I knew that I would have to make the attempt. Outside, the sun grew into the sky, spilling light across my path.

Petals open, birds sing, I coil. . .

NINE

Tick—I felt for the computer, reaching toward its innards, the sense of its constant operations coming to me as the extremities of waves touch the feet, barely, softly—*etder*—upon the beach. Then, striding ahead, their force growing upon my legs—*icketder*—I moved out toward the point of strongest impact, where—

Swerving, not slowing, moving like a deranged elephant, a huge truck in the near lane upon the opposite side of the highway left the road and bounced across the median strip, headed directly toward me.

My reaction was slow, since I had already begun my engagement with the computer. I lunged across the cab into the driver's seat, using the steering wheel to pull myself into place, my feet groping for the pedals. I sought frantically after the mechanism

which would switch my truck's control to manual,
since it seemed to be taking no action to avoid the
oncoming vehicle.

But I was not fast enough. It was upon me and—
gone.

I checked the side-mirror. I listened for the crash.
A pair of negatives. It had simply ceased to be, as if it
had been silently vaporized. A phantom.

I sniffed the air, suddenly suspicious. No. No floral
aromas had accompanied it. But it was the sort of
thing that Ann could have managed, and I couldn't
think of any other explanation.

I waited. I sat there leaning upon the wheel,
watching the road. If one had that effect on me,
where were the others? It wasn't like Ann to be
skimpy in these matters. A whole convoy ought to be
headed toward me by now.

Unless it were indeed something else. A holo-
gram? No. It was just too damned substantial, and I
couldn't see how that pinpoint accuracy and timing
could be achieved, anyway, in the absence of a lot of
complicated projection equipment. I looked sky-
ward. There were no hovering 'copters. Anyhow, I
didn't see how they could have located me to set the
thing up.

I waited. I sniffed. Nothing happened.

All right, then. I had a job to do.

Ticketder—I was back where I had been, bright
lights now gleaming beneath the waters like the
sunken city of Ys. The ocean, I knew, represented the
data-net. I would swim into that city. . .

. . . Rushing toward me, driving on the wrong
side of the road, a bright red sports car, moving at an
incredible speed—

My fingers tightened upon the wheel. My left foot automatically fell heavily upon the disengaged brake.

I did not remove myself from the computer, however. I moved immediately to monitor the radar unit, and I saw that, despite the evidence of my eyes, there was nothing there. There was not a trace of that small vehicle present.

And it, too, passed away. One moment it was before me, the next it was not.

—*rick*.

The hell with it then. If whatever game was being played was ultimately this harmless, then it did not warrant my attention.

Back to Ys.

I began my plunge.

No! Another truck! Only I could not be certain about this one for several moments. It overtook me on the left and moved to cut in far too soon. This seemed a possibly genuine thing, until the radar assured me that it was another ghost.

I began to grow angry. Despite their unreality, the things kept distracting me from the task at hand. They broke my concentration, they set me back. . .

And more than that. There was something about traffic accidents that I found extremely unsettling. I mopped my brow on the back of a trembling hand. I could worry about the why of it later. Right now I wanted to rid myself of the assaults. Even if I closed my eyes, I would be aware of their presence, as I had been of the illusions during my flight. But in this case, the awareness would be sufficient. They were touching upon some traumas I was not all that eager to unearth at the moment.

I sniffed again. No. But it did not matter. It had to be her.

"Ann?" I said aloud. "Why are you doing this to me, Ann? Didn't we used to be . . . friends? I seem to remember . . . The Boss can't possibly know that you've found me, that you're reading me—yet. Give me a break, will you? There's something I have to do. I'm not out to hurt Barbeau, to hurt Angra. I just want Cora back, and they've got her. If you want to tell them something about me, tell them that if they let me have her I'll go away and they'll never hear from me again. I mean it. You're the telepath, look in my mind and see if I don't mean it. Lay off on the trucks, will you? They're getting in my way."

An odor of violets seemed to fill the cab.

"Okay?" I said. "Please? Just give me some time for the things I have to do. I'd do it for you. Hold off."

The aroma persisted. There was no reply, but no new vehicles were rushing toward me either. I couldn't tell whether she was thinking about what I'd said or just biding her time for another onslaught.

But waiting would solve nothing, I decided after several minutes. Tentatively, I began the Coil Effect again.

Clickterclick. Tick. Derick.

Down. Through the clear, gleaming water, turning even as I passed into some more tenuous substance, arrays of lights hovering like disciplined squadrons of not-water fishes . . . Moving, threading my way among blazing columns, along snaking cables . . . There was a fascination here. There always was, but this was something different. Something stronger.

More than fascination. There was a sense of expectancy rising within me, anticipation . . . Something was different about my continents'-spanning microworld, and it almost seemed as if I should know what it was. But I did not. I continued to the point of passage to the larger system—a place of spark-emitting narrowness between a pair of glistening walls, darkness beyond. . .

"Yes." A reply within my mind, which I read in Ann's voice. And all of the overtones which accompanied it. She was going to give me my break. But not just to be nice. I could feel her presence strongly now. I could feel the fascination she felt for the phenomenon she was witnessing within my mind. She followed me down the slow spirals that began beyond the shining walls. Something inexplicable seemed to be impending, for the network held my mind in such a grip as it had never seemed to possess before. I felt that it was also holding Ann's mind in the same fashion.

Moving, around, around . . . A terminal . . . Through it . . . Another . . . Up and down . . . Now the wild roller coaster effect. . .

Ann was like a child, clinging to my back. I felt her fear. I also felt a powerful curiosity, almost a longing.

Turn, turn aside . . . Something . . . Summoning. . .

No!

Something, something out there . . . Calling, beckoning . . . I wanted to break my journey and go to it, but the thought of Cora, of my mission, made me resist, made me fight what was rapidly becoming an obsession. Something. . .

I tore my mind away, shaking free. I knew my goal. I could not afford to be turned from it. I plunged ahead. . .

. . . And Ann plunged with me.

"Turn!" I felt her say within my mind.

In that moment, I realized that the summons which I had ignored still held her. She wanted to travel that byway, trace it to its source.

I did not reply. Some things about Ann were coming back to me as I spiraled with the current, rising and falling at dizzying velocities. . .

Although I knew that she could see into my mind, I could not prevent myself from laying out some of the things about her which now returned to me. I could even feel her reactions as I did this.

I was still hazy as to how we had met, while I was back at the university. It seemed that I had learned of her powers at a fairly early point, though. They were potent. She might have carved some sort of empire for herself, rather than helping Barbeau to build his own. What could be safe from her mental probing if she'd a desire to know it? Who could long stand the hallucinatory stresses, the mental harassment she could bring to bear? She could learn secrets, displace enemies . . . she was a one-woman intelligence agency.

But.

She'd a weakness. A big one. Dependency. She kept it well masked, but she needed someone. She had always needed a strong personality outside herself to cling to.

Ahead . . . We were coming to something now. I

perceived it as a moat of fire. . .

Slow, now . . . Brake. Hold it. I was nearing my destination.

I felt Ann's excitement growing. I sensed her pique at my appraisal of her weakness. But I also sensed acknowledgement that it was correct. Barbeau provided the rock she clung to now, which was the reason she had tried to confuse me, to finish me off. She had wanted to get back in his good graces again after having failed to keep me in the Keys or break me down on the plane.

Steady . . . I drew nearer. Yes. I was moving about the peripheries of Angra's data-banks now. A dark form became apparent within the circle of fires. It grew even as I considered it, its outlines becoming more distinct. Dark, rough-hewn walls, notched as for battle, forms passing to and fro along them. Turrets, machicolated balconies. .

Big Mac was taking form as a fortress, a great, dark citadel within my mind's eye. Now lights flashed within a series of tiny oblong windows, giving to one wall the momentary impression of an old data-punched card held up to a bright light source. . .

Circling . . . Beyond Phlegethon's blaze, another wall became a scarred, unhuman, sculpted face. I reverberated within the circuit and studied it from several angles at once.

Now, a Stonehenge beneath the sea, filigrees of weeds swaying like smoke-plumes about it, luminescent barnacles winking on and off across its surfaces . . . Here, a nighted skyline within a massive box, filled with internal movement . . . There, an ominous black altar. . .

Fortress . . . Castle . . . Citadel . . . Pulsing, elemental servitors guarding its ramparts. . .

I continued to reverberate, dividing, multiplying my points of view. I had been within those storm-guaged walls before. Time was when I was welcome there. To cross over now, I must find its weaknesses. . .

I saw that no defender might leave its station. . .

Ann's presence continued to intrude, if only in the form of thoughts about her. Had I once been the strong personality to which she had clung? How had I come to work for Angra? Had these things been somehow connected?

And even as they ran through my mind, I felt these speculations—perhaps unwillingly—affirmed within Ann's consciousness, across the tenuous interface we shared.

The fires . . . The fires now claimed my attention, resolving themselves into internal, myriad, microscopic movements . . . The petals of flame became a pointillist study, discrete bright units becoming more and more apparent . . . Further, further—to their almost but not quite Brownian dartings. . .

And Ann, Ann was peering over my figurative shoulder as I carried out my probing. I could feel her wonder at the display. She could not see these things on her own. It was apparently worth the one drawback to her—namely, that I could sense certain things within her mind as well, when we were in such close proximity.

No, it was not really a random movement of the fiery particles . . . There was a rhythm, a definite periodicity, which, from my many points of view, now became apparent. Somewhere beyond, I was certain, lay word

*of Cora, information concerning her whereabouts. I
studied the movement more closely. . .*

I sensed an affirmative acknowledgement from
Ann when I thought of Cora.

"Where is she?" I queried. "If you know, tell me
and save me this trouble."

But I immediately sensed a negative. With some
difficulty, she covered over a thought of Cora in a
warm climate which was not that of Florida. I saw
that Ann was with me mainly for the spectacle. She
wanted to observe what I had done so far and what I
was about to attempt, for her own pleasure and
excitement. She could always withdraw in an instant if something horrible happened to me. Sec-
ondarily, she wanted to know it for certain if I did
not succeed—to have something to take back to
Barbeau, having failed in her latest attempt to do
me in or drive me over the edge with her illusions.
She would not willingly give anything away to
me.

"All right," I said. "Maybe voyeurism's better
than no passion at all."

A wave of pain, offended dignity and something
else passed over me. I ignored it and pressed ahead
on all fronts.

*. . . Continuing to reverberate at many points about
the moat, I moved forward until I was all but embrac-
ing the defending movements of the fiery particles.
Then I willed that they part before me. . .*

*The flames separated like opening beaks before all of
my posts of observation . . . I passed within.*

*The walls, at this range, seemed smoky, swirling,
flowing. . .*

I advanced at two points and was repulsed . . . The smokes had rushed together and taken on solid form before me, becoming some glistening substance—like blocks of black ice . . . Staring, I could discover crystal lattices within them, retreating into dark infinities. . .

. . . But as the forces of the citadel were mustered to repel the two aspects of myself, I noted that the walls weakened, growing more tenuous before me at the other vantages I occupied. . .

. . . And for a single, swimming moment they became again the walls which had resisted me when I had traced my check, the walls which then seemed to guard the lost log of my days . . . Somehow this was much less important to me now. Better now, I decided, to concentrate on my single objective. . .

I advanced at four points, and everything which remained before me was transformed into a swarm of fireflies, rushing to block me there. . .

I advanced at three more points, and at one of them I stepped through. . .

. . . into another city of lights—a Paris, a New York among computers: huge, brilliant, in motion at every point. . .

. . . A faceless phalanx of incandescent defenders rushed toward me, jerkily, like a grouping of marionettes. . .

I reverberated, until there were more of me than there were of them. Leaving my phase-doubles to combat them, with those portions of my consciousness committed there, I pressed ahead. . .

. . . to see that if I were to completely suppress the defenders in that place, a soundless alarm would divert

*a river of light which flowed to my left, causing it to
flow to my right. . .*

*. . . and if this occurred, I would be barred from
entering a maze-like grid. It would cover it over, ruin-
ing the next stage of my journey. . .*

*. . . so I deviated, heading for the place of the alarm.
To tamper with it, however, I saw, would cause the grid
itself to flip, closing down a part of the system. . .*

*. . . but then there was the mechanism itself which
would cause the flipping. It could be deactivated by
means of a coded command, the template for which
hovered near the alarm like a holographic negative
hole-in-space. . .*

*Back-reading, I found the code, then deactivated the
alarm . . . In each of my other phases, I was holding
one of the incandescent defenders at bay . . . For a
nanosecond or so, I saw superimposed scenes of the
storming of a castle from some medieval epic on the
Late Late Show, my subconscious stirred by some
vaguely poetic impulse now it was feeling its oats.*

*. . . Torches, cries, flames, flashing blades, buckets
of gore, bits of armor here and there, the neighing of a
horse, arrow-pierced cuirasses. Alarms and excur-
sions. . .*

*I shook off the illusions without shedding all of the
excitement. I regarded the grid, knowing I had to enter
there, knowing too that if I proceeded incorrectly the
Double Z data I sought would be shifted, dispersed, to
other locales in the overall system, necessitating my
hunting them down again—and being faced with the
same problem. The data would flee and continue to
flee, finding new hiding places, unless it were approached in the proper fashion. . .*

Another template hovered nearby, but when I back-read it, it provided no key. I studied it, puzzled . . . It looked almost useful. Then I realized that it spoke my old language, deceit. I saw that it had to be inverted. I did this. Then I superimposed its pattern upon the grid and it was like staring simultaneously through the scopes of a whole battery of rifles—the crosshaired cells indicating the pattern of entry. . .

I matched myself to the pattern—like patching a section of wallpaper—and slipped through. . .

. . . into a multilevel maze. It was like moving through a kind of phase space, but the dimensionality was not that important a part of it. I was aware that my understanding of the situation would persist for so long as I was a part of the process. Afterwards, I knew that I would recall it less clearly. My power did not function in a vacuum; it required a situation against which to react. My awareness which accompanied its direction found some means of comprehending the situation, if only by functional analogy. . .

. . . therefore, I saw myself/selves moving simultaneously through several levels of the maze. At each junction, it was necessary to pluck and back-read the template coding for the program I was following—somewhat more complicated than an on-off choice, as I had passed through a binary-quaternary converter on breaching this level of the system itself; a later addition, I decided, installed for greater economy of memory, but also situated where it was as an additional security baffle. . .

I wormed my way through the grid's mazework, overflashed once with another combative construct . . . Fighting in rush-strewn, tapestried halls, stone-

walled and gray. . . Screams and wailing . . . Heavy, dark-wooden furniture . . . A swaying candelabra . . . Dogs barking. . .

. . . I emerged into a mall-like area, parallel rows of lights racing off before me toward some hopefully less than infinite vanishing point . . . I felt myself growing tired as I regarded them. The struggle with Big Mac's defenses was beginning to fray my concentration. . .

I could feel Ann's rapt attention. She was impressed by what she had seen, though her comprehension lagged behind the sensations themselves. She seemed almost to be urging me to produce more spectacles for her.

"I should charge you admission," I said in my mind, and I felt something like amusement in response.

. . . I suggested to my subconscious that another analogue might come in handy. Immediately, the prospect before me began to waver and shift. . .

. . . I stood in a seemingly infinite library. Lines of stacks ran on and on and on before me, into the distance. I moved among them. . .

"Don't let it be the Dewey Decimal System," I warned my subconscious—long having suspected it of possessing a twisted sense of humor, I realized at that moment.

I hurried forward. The rows were labelled alphabetically, huge metal letters affixed at the foot of each. . .

. . . A, B. . .

C!

. . . I turned and moved up C. The Ca's seemed to go on for forever. I felt my mental fatigue increasing. The

long shelves of elaborately bound books seemed determined to hold the Ca range. I began to run. . .

. . . From somewhere in the distance, my mind supplied the sounds of continuing conflict within the huge central donjon—moving nearer. I was simultaneously aware, in my other forms, that the tide of battle was shifting—that I might be losing my grip on one of the alarm systems which I was simply holding in abeyance, like the jaws of a spring-steel trap. To add a touch of the olfactory, my subconscious threw in a smell of smoke. . .

"Thanks, subconscious," I growled, mentally. . .

. . . I finally made it to the Ce's—another interminable-seeming stretch. I increased my pace. I felt Ann's excitement continuing to rise in direct proportion to my own distress. It was still moot as to whether she was cheering me on or hoping to witness an unhappy ending in spades. . .

I threw extra strength into my reverberant-attackers' struggle against the defenders. As I did so, the titles beside me became harder to read. Smoke drifted past me, slid between me and the shelves, curled before the lettering upon the spines. . .

Cursing, I slowed and read. Still in the Ce's. Damn!

On and on I ran. The floor became a mirror, and then the ceiling did. An infinite race of BelPatris hurrying through the smoke of reality, the past ablaze to the rear, the future an uncertain progression to infinity. The race is not always to the swift, but that's the way to bet. Damon Runyon? Yes . . . I felt something like laughter—my own—within and about me. It frightened me. . .

I checked the shelves again. Ch's now, thank God!

Next the Ci's, and then. . .

Ci's! I was into them almost before I knew it. Who needs Ci's? I'd a mind to dump the entire Ci section of Big Mac's memory here in Double Z, as an act of protest or revenge. I also realized that I was suffering from an increasing irrationality from the strain.

. . . The clash of arms grew louder, the smells stronger. The smoke thickened. . .

No!

I could not let go at this point! Not this near to my goal!

I struggled to reassert my control, to affirm my supremacy over all of the systems which confronted me. I slowed. I focussed my concentration. . .

The smoke began to dissipate, the sounds grew fainter, the books seemed more solid, their titles clearer—

Co! I was into the Co's!

I almost lost control again at the realization. But the infinite clan of BelPatris—both upside-down and rightside-up—got hold of itself, stabilized its unimaginatively repetive environment and continued through the Cob's and the Cod's. . .

Col's. . .

Com's. . .

Con's, too. And after the Cop's and Coq's came Cora, coming cunningly, contiguous, constant Cora, Cora consolidated, contained, capsulized, captioned, captured—captive Cora!—concommitant Cora, Cora culled and collected, copyright Cora closed close, covered—

I dragged my mind back from the Joycean power of the C-matrix and grasped at the Cora volume. Already *the smoke was returning, at my brief interval of distraction. The sounds and the smells were rising again, the balance tipping once more in Big Mac's favor. . .*

I opened the blue-leather, gold-stamped volume. . .

Cora read the title page, fading even as I regarded it. . .

. . . Cora, still safe, in the hot Southwest . . . Cora, in . . . New Mexico? Arizona? "Southeastern quadrant of that section of northernmost New Spain. . ."

"New Mexico." Ann could not hide the thought from me in her excitement at witnessing a problem almost solved—the universal impulse to kibitz—"near Carlsbad".

Smoke billowed up about me. I let go the jaws of the trap. My troops retreated. . .

Careless now, I rushed away, leaving Big Mac to scream and gnash his teeth. . .

Ann, shocked, recovered in a moment with something almost like a sob. She went her way and I went mine. . .

Somewhere along the homeward trail, I sensed the shadowy presence once again. This time it did not beckon. . .

"Top of the morning to you," I broadcast. "Let's get together for lunch sometime."

. . . And then the spiral.

I opened my eyes for a few moments. Bright daylight flooded the cab. The truck's speed was undiminished. I thought I had what I wanted, but I did not feel like sorting through it all and making plans.

A certain numbness had come to fill my head, slowing the thinking machinery.

I closed my eyes again, to dream I was the cargo of
a coffin on wheels, and other things. . .

TEN

. . . Were driving. A long stretch of Texas highway . . . I was reading a book in the rear seat.
Nevertheless, I was peripherally aware of the deso-
late countryside, bleaker now beneath mountains of
clouds than it had been when we had commenced
this journey. Aware, too, of the heavy crosswinds,
gusts of which occasionally slammed our light
car—blows from the palm of a giant hand. The
thunder was long, deep rumbles somewhere in the
distance, considerably later than the flashes which
crawled like rivulets of molten gold spilled from the
heights, the cloud-peaks . . . The sound of a horn
dopplered toward us and passed. Dad was driving.
My mother was in the front passenger seat. The
radio was playing softly, a Country and Western
station . . . I was home for a brief holiday, and we
were on our way to visit Dad's older brother's fam-

ily. I had a lot of studying to do, though, and the books were stacked on the seat at my side. The first drops of rain hit the rooftop like bullets, and shortly after that I heard the windshield wipers come on. The guitar and the familiar nasal twang of someone singing about cheatin' and drinkin' and sneakin' around and not havin' any fun doin' it was interrupted with greater and greater frequency by bursts of static, unless it was the irate husband shootin' at him. In either case, my mother switched it to an FM station where the music was all instrumental and less strenuous. A car passed us, going pretty fast, and I heard Dad mutter something as he put the lights on. Another slap of the giant hand and Dad twisted the wheel to bring us back off of the shoulder. A clap of thunder seemed to come from directly overhead, and a moment later the rain came down like a waterfall. I closed the book, holding my place with a finger, and looked outside. Heavy, gray, beaded curtains cut visibility to a few car-lengths. The wind began screaming at us between buffets. "Paul," my mother said, "maybe you'd better pull over . . ." Dad nodded, glanced at the rear and sideview mirrors, peered ahead. "Yeah," he said then, and he began to turn the wheel. As he did, another gust struck us. We were on the shoulder and then beyond it. He'd hit the brakes and we were skidding. My stomach twisted as we suddenly nosed downward. A scraping noise passed beneath me, and I heard my mother scream, "No!" Then we were falling, and I heard a crash that was thunder and one that was not thunder, smothering the music and my mother's final scream and everything else. . .

I screamed. My eyes opened wide—unseeing for several moments—moist . . . It had been a dream, but it had been more than a dream. It was something that had really happened. It was how my parents had died. It was—

There was a star-shaped hole in the windshield and we were drifting gently to the right. My real-life truck was in the process of doing the same thing that had happened . . . nine years ago . . . though there was no storm, no deep arroyo near the road. A cornfield invited me to wallow amid its green ranks. . .

I catapulted myself into the driver's seat, this time locating the switch for manual operation quickly, having intentionally noted its placement in the wiring scheme that last time I'd coiled through the onboard computer.

I twisted almost savagely into the computer again, simultaneous with turning the wheel and pulling back onto the highway. The sideview showed the truck behind me dropping back. The one ahead pulled forward. The dance without the dancer. . .

There were other holes—they had to be bulletholes—which I could see now had stitched the truck's body, forward and to the left. Little whistling noises filled the cab. A greater, thrumming noise moved through the air overhead.

My coil-scan showed me that the computer had been damaged. I had to keep it on manual if I wanted to keep it on the road.

The thrumming sound grew louder, and the shadow of the helicopter passed—something like a piece of the night.

Then I saw it, and I heard the gunfire. I felt the impacts as the slugs tore into my truck. I smelled hot oil.

I was out of the truck's computer by then and reaching, reaching . . . Up, high . . . Trying to feel the computer that ran the 'copter's autopilot. . .

I felt stupid. I had thought I'd done such a clever thing in altering the truck's identification code. I had been tired, I had been wrapped up in the joy of self-discovery over the new aspect of my power, but still—

I had stupidly thought to hide myself by that single change of code. If anything, it had made me more vulnerable. I was probably part of a convoy—I hadn't even bothered to check—with maybe a couple of dozen of us all headed for Memphis from the same warehouse or factory somewhere in the East. Mine—whatever its number in line—might as well have had a red X painted on its roof. I should have checked first and then altered the descriptions of the whole lot of us. Barbeau hadn't even needed Ann's efforts against me. Without any special skills, he had beaten me at my own game. I should have foreseen it. I should have. . .

Up, reaching . . . I felt it now, the autopilot's brain. I coiled into it and began a rapid scan of its systems as the pilot circled to come at me again. In the meantime, I smelled smoke and my engine was starting to make funny noises; there were intermittent hesitations. . .

The 'copter swooped in, and I seized the autopilot controls and activated them, trying to drive it off course to the right. . .

The helicopter jerked just as a gun began to flash,

forward. The firing stopped immediately. The shots went wide.

The 'copter commenced a little dance. Wisps of smoke were now drifting past me, there in the driver's seat. I felt a warmth near my right foot. My engine coughed. The truck stalled and pulled out of it, stalled and pulled out of it. . .

Overhead, the 'copter veered to the right, corrected and then was gone as I flashed by beneath it. I could feel the pilot struggling with the controls, fighting the automatic system which had come awake to oppose him. I continued my efforts, striving to sweep the vehicle away, downward. . .

The thrumming faded, grew again. I watched the road's shoulder, unable to see my attacker. It came into sight on my far left. The fact that its pilot was trying to kill me had only gradually sunk to the gut level where fear, hate and all of the survival instincts are stored. My heart was pounding. I began to cough as the smoke thickened within the cab. We were past the cornfields now and into an area of rolling terrain. I reasserted the autopilot's program for sweeping off to my right, sinking.

The sounds of its engine laboring, the 'copter began to do just that. I could feel the force of the struggle quite clearly—machine against man, me on the side of the former. Gun forgotten, the pilot was fighting with his controls now. I countered his every move. The 'copter heeled over and plunged toward the earth.

I didn't really see it happen. I think I was more than partway past when it hit, and the smoke had continued to thicken within the cab. By the time that I got the window open there were flames inside with me. It was a peculiar feeling, though . . . Whoever had piloted the thing was just a faceless abstraction to me, someone wishing me ill, not that I was eager to see anyone dead . . . But the computer—

I had been inside it. I had just gotten acquainted. And then I had forced it to operate to its own destruction. I had been inside of it at the crash, also, when its systems went wild and then stopped. I felt a small twinge of guilt then, even though there was no true sentience involved. When is a thing not a thing?

I began to go off the road once more. I turned the steering wheel again and it did not respond. I hit the brakes. They weren't working either.

The truck kept right on going, off of the road, down a slope, headed toward a large outcropping of stone toward the center of the field. Was I irrational at that point? Probably somewhat. I coiled into my truck's computer and it was dead, save for a couple of maintenance systems which were in maximum trouble. I had a feeling that this was it, with Ann not even there to enjoy my passing. Though maybe she wouldn't have . . . I wasn't certain. Once she had liked me. I was sure of that now. We *had* actually meant something to each other, it seemed, somewhere along the line. . .

Just in case, Ann . . . I thought then, with special emphasis. *Just in case . . . this is it . . . and I think it is . . . I know that The Boss got me here from the machines, not from you . . . Smell your flowers . . . If you hear me now, it's not the way I want to go—if I have to—but I know this one isn't yours . . . I won't go cursing you, for just keeping me company awhile—despite your Grade B illusions . . . I wish I remem-*

*bered more, though . . . You're the only one who
might . . . hear me now . . . and I'll give you a good-
bye on that. You could have done better than Barbeau,
though. Smell your damn flowers, lady. . .*

. . . And then the engine sounds grew louder and
louder and louder—until I realized that they were
not all my engine sounds. I felt the presence of other
functioning computer systems nearby. Then came
the shadows. And the jolt.

I was sweating and choking and full of panic, but
as the shadows paced me and the first one made
contact I understood.

Two other trucks had left the highway, pursued
me, caught up with me, were pacing me. The one to
the right had just made contact, with a grinding
sound. Now I felt the impact of the one on the left.
Metal screeched and buckled and fragments of my
dream shot like meteors through my head, trailing
fear in their wake.

A change of perspective . . . Flames heavy now
. . . But I was no longer headed downhill. I was
being turned. Like a pair of elephants helping a
wounded comrade, the two trucks were redirecting
my course, turning me away from the crash that
waited at the hill's foot.

It gave me a few moments more, but it was still no
good. The flames were going to get me very soon. I
was going to have to get out. That meant jumping,
and I knew that jumping at this speed would kill me.

I looked to my left. The truck on that side was no
longer in contact. The one of the right was pushing,
herding me now. Only a meter and a half, perhaps,
separated me from the vehicle to the left. Its door
had even sprung when it had ground against my

truck. It was partway open, perhaps wedged in that position.

A leap across. If I could make it . . . I had to make it. It was the only way open to me, the only chance to go on living.

I swung my door open, holding it against the wind, edging myself around on the seat, facing outward. At the rush of air, flames leaped at my back, singed my garments. I looked downward and that was a mistake. I tore my gaze away to stare once again at the racing sanctuary, so near. What was I waiting for? Just to let the fear eat away at my resolve? There was really no choice. I made up my mind exactly where I would grab hold.

I leaped.

* * *

. . . Pouring rain. The grating noise that passed beneath me as we nosed downward . . . My mother's scream . . . The thunder and the crash . . . Blackness that went on and on and on and would not go away—oh, no!—forever. . .

Blackness.

Silence.

Blackness and silence.

And in the midst of these, pain. My head. . .

The pain lessened at intervals and my mind floated—a kind of drunken, disengaged feeling. Not unpleasant, for anything which kept thinking at arms' length was welcome.

I seemed to be lying on my back somewhere, though I could not be absolutely certain. I possessed no particular sensations save for the pain and that feeling of position. Later, though, it felt as if my head were resting upon a pillow.

I tried to cry out. I heard nothing.

A sense of profound wrongness had been with me for a long while.

How long?

Days? Weeks? I had no idea, save that it was no short interval.

My thoughts drifted back to the crash, over and over again. Was this death—consciousness drifting in a dark, silent void, still bearing the pains of its passing? There were times when I believed this. Other times, I felt something like an unseen hand upon my brow.

See?

Could it be that I had been blinded? Deafened, too, possibly? The thoughts made me want to scream. If I did, it was like that tree falling in the forest for me.

Blackness and silence.

Gradually, the pain subsided. By then, I had been through periods of panic and nightmare irrationality, of despondency, lethargy, despair. There were times when I could not draw the line between waking and sleeping. I knew who I was, but I did not know where or when I was.

What changed all of this was the food. Why should a disembodied spirit want or need food? My mouth was opened gently, and a bit of broth—from a squeeze-bottle, it seemed—came into it. I gagged. I choked for awhile, but finally I got some down.

That moment marked my certainty that I was in a hospital bed—blind, deaf and paralyzed. It is strange that such a horrible realization should be, however briefly, accompanied by a feeling of relief. But at least I knew where I was, and that I was being cared for. All of my dark metaphysical speculations fled. I was alive and being treated. I could now begin hoping for recovery. . .

I marked the passage of time by my feedings. I put off thinking about the accident for as long as I could. But eventually I came to dwell upon it.

Were my parents alive or dead? Were we in beds but a short distance apart, or . . . If they were alive, were their conditions anything like my own? I thought about the car's plunge again and again. I might have done better than they did by virtue of having occupied the back seat. Or, the car might have done a complete flip, leaving me the worst off.

Pure morbidity, when I had no way of checking on these matters. But I couldn't help it. I sought after other things to occupy my mind. I thought about school, about the exams I would doubtless miss— had probably already missed. I ran through a typical day on campus, trying to recall everyone I knew there. I tried to remember the placement of everything in my room. I recalled some of the better lectures I had heard, books I had read. . .

I made up mental games and played them. I got so that I could visualize a chessboard pretty well, but it was no fun with no real opponent. . .

And whenever I paused, my ingenuity exhausted the sleep still far away, I eventually began wondering whether I might not be better off dead. If I lacked much in the way of bodily sensations I had probably suffered some damage to my brain or spinal cord. I knew that this was not good at all if I didn't begin recovering some feelings soon. Those head pains had been fierce. I missed the don't-give-a-damn feeling the narcotics had induced earlier. And there were times when I wondered whether I might be going crazy—or might not already have done so.

I tried speaking. Whether I could hear it or not was immaterial, if someone else could. I tried saying, "My head hurts" over and over again. It didn't, really, anymore. But someone must have heard and given me a shot of something to take away my pain. I drifted again.

I tried it frequently after that, but it only worked a few more times. They must have caught on. But it gave me an idea.

The next time that I felt a hand on my forehead, I tried to say, "Wait. Am I in a hospital? Press once if I am, twice if I'm not."

The fingertips pressed once.

"My parents," I said. "Are they alive?"

There was a hesitation. I knew what that meant even before I felt the answer that finally came.

I went into some sort of withdrawal after that. Maybe I did go crazy for awhile.

Later—days later, possibly—I came around. I tried again.

When I felt the hand, ignored so often now, I asked, "Is my spinal cord severed?"

Two touches.

"Is it damaged?"

One touch.

"Will I get better?"

Nothing. Wrong phrasing, I guessed.

"Is there a chance I'll get better?"

Hesitation. One touch.

Not too promising.

"Are my eyes damaged?"

Two touches.

"Is it my brain?"

One touch.

"Can it be remedied?"

No touches.

"Would surgery help?"

No touches. Had my respondent left? Wait—

"Have I already had surgery?"

One touch.

"How soon till we know whether it was effective?"

No touches.

"Shit," I said, and I withdrew again. I couldn't think of anything else to ask. Those were all of the things that mattered to me. I felt the hand very many times again, but I just didn't know what else to say.

There followed long intervals during which I must have been psychotic, times full of weird dream-like sequences that were not dreams, just mental wanderings. In between, there were some lucid spells. During one of the later ones I decided to try to preserve my sanity. Why, I am not certain. Maybe the decision was a mad act in itself. It could be that I'd be better off if I lost all touch with reason, abandoned any sense of self. Yet, I decided to try holding myself together against the chaos.

I began by telling myself my life story. Broad and sketchy at first, I began delving for more and more detail. I went back as far as I could. I worked my way slowly forward, many times. I conjured up the faces of my classmates in elementary school, searching for names for each of them. I remembered tablecloths and rugs and pictures on walls that I hadn't

thought of in years. Every relative, every friend . . .
The clothing I had worn at different times . . . My
first fight, my first crush . . . Every injury. I thought
of Christmases and Thanksgivings and birthdays,
seating arrangements at dinners, presents given and
received, marriages, births, deaths . . . My parents'
business . . . It occupied me for a long while. I was
surprised at all the things which lay just out of sight
in memory. . .

My parents' business?

I remembered the computers and the games that I
used to play with them. I thought about each one
that I had known, many of them personified, just as I
had thought about my classmates.

I even remembered the time when I thought that I
had somehow seen into the workings of that one. . .

I found myself wishing that I had a computer to
talk with again.

And I thought once more about that strange feeling, forgotten all these years.

Click. Click. Click. Derick. Yes. Like that. And
then. . .

. . . *It was rows and rows of lights and spinning
hoops of fire. I followed a bright spiral through a
crackling, clicking wonderland.* . .

It was like going back. This was the feeling. Only
this was not the same machine, resurrected in memory. It was a real, nearby computer that I was looking into. I was certain. How, or exactly where, I
could not for a moment tell. But I sensed the transactions of data about me, the messages coming
clearer and clearer as I regarded the phenomenon. . .

I had somehow made contact with the hospital's computer. I was into its workings, a silent partner, observing. Suddenly, I was no longer alone.

Every day then, upon awakening, I fled, coiled, into that wonderful machine. It became my friend. There were data, data and more data to hold my interest. I dismissed any shadowy desire to communicate further with those who fed, bathed and medicated me. I knew all their names now—who was on duty, who off—and something of their life-histories, from their personnel files. I read all of the menus in advance. I reviewed all of the other patients' records—as well as my own. I was in bad shape, with a totally pessimistic prognosis. I discovered that anything I did not understand in the way of medical terminology could be learned via the linkage with the medical library computer. I knew where all of my bedsores were located, even though I could not feel them. I was depressed at my findings as to my own case. Still, I had this much which I had not had before, a window onto the world.

And as entries were dated, I became aware of the passage of time once again. Days and weeks fled, turned into months. My window grew in size, became a vast, panoramic screen. . .

The hospital computer was connected to a police computer, the medical library computer was connected to a university computer, the university computer was connected to a military computer, the military computer was connected to a meteorological computer—like the man said about bones. And along the way, there were bank computers, think tank computers, private computers, linkages to foreign computers. . .

I could range the world. I could keep posted on the news. I could read books, locate facts in an instant, spectate at all manner of games and real-life situations. . .

I learned to ride the flux. *Clickaderick.*

Of course it mattered that my body lay numb and useless. But at least I was a part of the world again. I had structures to cling to, fascinating things to observe. I could lose myself for days at a time following business or political or military manipulations of people and things and monies . . . I watched corporate takeovers, economic sanctions in tricky political situations, negotiations for a major league player trade, the restructuring of a university from a liberal arts to a technical institution. I predicted a suicide, I foresaw an oceanographic concern's rise to prominence, I witnessed the recovery of a lost satellite. I was no longer lonely. I wanted my body back again, functioning properly, but at least I no longer felt the dissolving touch of madness. . .

I wondered—of course I wondered—as to the nature of my bond with the machines. I'd never heard or read of anything like it. It seemed like a bizarre form of telepathy—human to machine. I tried on a number of occasions to read the minds of the people who moved about me, and I was totally unsuccessful. It appeared that my ability was very specialized. I realized that I must have been born with some small aptitude along these lines, and that it might never have developed further but for the unique set of circumstances into which I had been thrust.

Whatever its genesis and method, I could not but be grateful. Other patients, in better shape, might have television sets in their rooms. I had a connection with much of the world right there in my head.

. . . And more time passed. The records showed that my condition was static. I remained underweight, catheterized, my bowels stimulated electrically. I occasionally required hookup to an IV, I received regular medication, I was manipulated and turned, but I still suffered from bedsores. Further surgery was not indicated. It was implied by one neurologist that I was probably totally psychotic by then, anyhow. From all indications, I was, and would remain, a vegetable for the rest of my days.

I tried to resign myself to this, but naturally it haunted my dreams and some intervals of wakefulness. I researched my condition, of course, but could find nothing too encouraging.

I continued to seek my diversion within the data-net, always alert for any medical breakthroughs which might bear upon my condition.

I do not know at exactly what point it was that I became vaguely apprehensive. Not about my condition. Nothing in my records indicated imminent death or a sudden downturn. No. While I had not exactly become stoical or in any way resigned to my fate, I nurtured some small hope of recovery, possessed some bit of wishful thinking that that medical breakthrough would come along and work my eventual recovery. I needed that much. The feeling is more difficult to explain. As I ranged through the data-net, I occasionally had the impression that someone was looking over my shoulder. At first, it was only a casual, intermittent thing, but later it came to me with greater and greater frequency. I dismissed it for a time as a form of paranoia. After all, my condition had certainly unbalanced me for a long while, and now my only form of recreation was of a highly unusual character. Being haunted by a ghost in the machine might well be a reaction—possibly even a healthy one, signifying that I was now turning my attention, actually seeking, for things beyond the ego-filled universe I had inhabited for so long. But it persisted, grew stronger and became for a time my constant companion. It seems that eventually I reached some accommodation with the feeling. I was not about to give up my pastimes. A certain haziness covers that period, however, a thing possibly connected with the events which followed.

I woke up one morning with some sensation in my left thigh. I could not move the leg, or anything that complicated, but the area—about the size of the palm of my hand—tingled; it burned. It became very uncomfortable and totally distracting. I could not coil away, I could not do anything but think about it—for hours, I guess. Strangely, it did not occur to me at first that this might be an encouraging sign. I simply looked upon it as a new torment. The next time that I awoke, I felt it in the toes of my left foot, also, with intermittent flashes of sensitivity in the calf; also, the area upon my thigh had grown larger. It struck me about then that something good might be happening.

The rest is a jumble, a montage—and it took place over a period of many weeks. I remember the terrible buzzing in my ears which went on for days and days before it resolved itself into discrete sounds and, later, words. I was barely aware of the faint light until I had been seeing it for more than a day. My right leg, my abdomen and my arms caught the fire and the itching, and finally I felt the pain of the bedsores. I forget at exactly what point it was that a nurse became aware of the change in my condition. Doctors came and went in great numbers, and I got to see and talk with that neurologist who'd thought I must have gone crazy. Needless to say, I did not tell him—or anyone else—about the Coil Effect, as I'd come to think of my pastimes, for fear of confirming him in the opinion.

It was a long time and much physiotherapy before I could walk again, but it was sufficient during the interval to be wheeled about the corridors and later to wheel myself, to be able to look out of windows at the grounds or the traffic, to talk with other patients. It was good to be able to feed myself. And I decided not to start smoking again, having gotten a complete, free withdrawal out of my former condition.

While my parents' deaths still pained me, and I knew that one of my first acts upon release would be to visit their graves, I had lived with the knowledge for a long while and it was no longer constantly on my mind.

The medical breakthrough I had awaited had not occurred. My body, with the passage of time, had fortunately been able to manage the remission on its own.

. . . And as I rested, I coiled, for now the computer connection had become a part of my life, was a phenomenon for which I felt a great affection. I was grateful that the ability had not left me, being somehow displaced by the return of my other faculties. I still ranged the data-net as I lay in bed in the evenings. But somehow it was no longer exactly the same.

Click.

* * *

I lay there, gasping, on the front seat of the truck which had come to my rescue. Already, it had slowed, dropped back and pulled away from my burning vehicle and the other rescuer, which had also taken fire. We were swinging back toward the road, climbing the slope now.

My back still felt hot. I reeked of smoke, mixed with the smell of singed hair and cloth. I tasted the smoke in my mouth. I coughed and drew deep breaths of this cleaner air. The partway opened door creaked as we hit a rut. Its window was cracked but not broken.

I elbowed myself upward and drew the sprung door more tightly closed. As I did, I saw my original transport and the other truck collide with the rocky outcrop at the field's center. A pair of explosions followed and the fires danced rings around the scene of carnage. The cracks in the glass flashed like lightning bolts as it happened.

ELEVEN

The other vehicles in the automated lane made room for us, and soon we were a part of the traffic flow once again. It was, of course, too good to last. We had broken the pattern of the traffic control computer's programming routine and must even now be showing up as an oddity. While I might have gotten away with reprogramming a long line of vehicles earlier, I was fairly certain that it wouldn't work now. There had to be some sort of alert in effect after the results of my last alteration had become known. And the vehicle I rode would even be easy to spot physically, with the damage it had sustained.

A quick coil, a quick search, showed me that I was in eastern Tennessee. I caused the truck to pull over onto the shoulder, and I ran it along there for nearly a mile before I stopped it and got out. Off in the distance, across open fields and better-groomed grounds, appeared what could be the line of a railroad track. Reaching out, I could feel the data-flow along the fiber-optic cables which followed it.

I stood beside the truck for a moment. Looking back, I could see the dark, wind-twisted streamers of smoke which rose from the wreckage of my original truck and its companion. I hoped that Barbeau would assume I had been killed in it, at least for a sufficient while to give me something of a headstart.

I instructed my rescuing vehicle to return to the automated lane and continue on its way. Obediently, the gears ground and it moved off, the other trucks immediately adjusting their spacing to accommodate its presence.

I checked the skies. There were no more 'copters in sight. I did, however, hear the sound of a distant siren. I commenced hiking across the green and hilly countryside, heading in the direction of the park-like expanse. There were a number of buildings in that area, though not a great deal of activity. I guessed, as I walked among reedy grasses over the red clodded earth, that it was probably a campus that I was approaching.

Rick. Click. Terick. Yes. There was a computer there, a list of grades within it. Summer session stuff.

Far away, the siren died. I believed that it had stopped in the area of the burning trucks. It would be some time, I decided, before they could really go through that smouldering wreckage. But I increased my pace through the midday heat. It would be pleasant to pass into the shade up ahead. I certainly looked presentable enough for a campus.

I found my way to a path which widened and acquired gravel as I progressed. I smelled magnolias and recently mown grass. Real smells—I could see the trees and the place where the lawn had been cut—not preface to some imaginary horrors.

Several guys and gals were tossing a frisbee in an open area to my right and ahead. They paid me no special attention. Passing them and approaching the buildings, I caught the smell of food and my stomach immediately began sending signals.

A flight of concrete stairs with a pipe railing led down to an opened door. Behind it was a small cafeteria-style lounge. I stood beside the doorway as if looking for someone. I noted that people were paying cash to the boy at the register, who was reading a paperback between customers. I saw no flashing of ID cards.

So I went in and passed along the line, buying two hot dogs, a bag of chips and a large Coke. I took them back outside with me to a secluded bench I had noted beneath a large old tree.

It was a peculiar feeling, sitting there and eating, watching students pass. It made me think of my own days in school. I was about to reach out for the computer again—just for company, I guess—when a girl in white shorts, a lime jersey and tennis shoes passed, a racquet in her hand. She descended the stairs into the eatery. About Ann's height and build, Same color hair.

. . . And she came walking through my memory, as she had that day on campus, wearing a white silk blouse and dark blue skirt, carrying a small purse. I was standing in the doorway of the Student Union, out of the wind. She looked right at me, as if she already knew who I was and smiled and named me. I nodded.

". . . And you are Ann Strong," I said.

"Yes," she replied. "I'd like to take you to lunch."

"All right."

I started to turn.

"Not in there," she said. "Someplace a bit more civilized, and quiet."

"Okay."

She had a car. She drove us to an off-campus place, the dining room at her venerable hotel, where the food was excellent and the napkins heavy cloth.

I had been back at school for over three months. It had been a little over twice that time between my recovery and my entering the university again. I had thrown myself into my studies as if they were occupational therapy, and I expected to do very well on my finals in a few weeks.

Our talk on the way over had been general, directed toward getting us acquainted. Nor did she rush into anything as we ate. I actually forgot briefly that she was a recruiter for Angra Energy, so pleasant was the conversation. She seemed to hit, as if by chance, upon nearly everything in which I was currently interested, even a couple of books which I had recently enjoyed or was just then reading.

Finally, as we sat drinking coffee, she asked me, "What sort of plans have you made for the future?"

"Oh, something having to do with computers," I replied.

"Would you consider going East?"

I shrugged.

"I hadn't really thought about it," I said. "If I liked a job I'd go wherever it took me."

"Well, you've come to my attention as a possibility for recruitment by Angra."

"That puzzles me," I replied. "I thought that you were only hiring graduating seniors and grad students. I'm not there yet."

She took a sip of coffee.

"I am here to look for talent," she said, "not for pieces of paper with fancy writing on them."

I smiled.

"But of course you want that, too."

"Not necessarily," she stated. "Not in special cases."

The waiter came by and refilled our cups. As I raised mine, Ann reached out and touched the rosebud in the cut glass vase between us.

"I am flattered by what I think you are saying," I finally answered, "but I doubt that I've been back in school long enough to provide much of a record for you to go on."

"I've seen your earlier records," she said, "and of course we are also influenced by current professors' recommendations."

"You know about the accident?"

"Yes."

"To be practical about it—from your point of view—it could have left me unbalanced. Would it not be more prudent to watch such a person for a longer period of time?"

She nodded.

"That is one of the arguments for personal contact. May I watch you?"

"Of course."

"*Are* you unbalanced?"

I laughed.

"Stable as a rock," I said.

"In that case, Angra's generous expense account

will include dinners. Would you be free Friday evening?"

"Yes."

"There is a play opening that night, which I would like to see."

"I like plays," I answered. "But I don't want to string you along under false pretenses. I really think that I want to finish school before I take a job."

She put her hand on my arm.

"We can talk about such matters another time," she replied. "But I should mention that Angra does provide opportunities for the continuing education of its employees. More importantly right now, I need justification to use the expense account myself. I'll pick you up at your place at six, on Friday."

"That'll be nice," I said.

And it was. She was going to be in town for an indeterminate period of time—at least several weeks, she told me—and there were lots of good things to see and do, if one had money and a car and wanted to get to know someone real well.

Even though we became lovers during the weeks which followed, I refused to leave school to take a job with Angra at the end of the mid-year semester. I was determined to complete the academic year and start work that summer. That way, I decided, if I did not like the job I would be able to quit and return in the fall without missing any time. It sounded, I suppose, presumptuous for an undergraduate offered a good position with a major company to dictate terms that way, but I was already beginning to suspect that my case involved something special. The fact that they agreed to my terms only seemed to confirm it.

And Ann was in and out of town constantly. That following semester I was seeing her just about every weekend. It was almost as if she were keeping some sort of watch over me. I even asked:

"You certainly make it through here a lot. Are they afraid some other company's going to steal me?"

She looked hurt.

"I juggle my schedule for you," she replied. "*Would* you go elsewhere if you suddenly had another offer?"

"I haven't had any," I told her. "But no, I said that I'd try it at Angra and I will."

"Then let us enjoy this bonus my travel permits."

It seemed almost ungracious to pursue matters beyond that. Yet, I realized that I was only one of many bright kids across the country. I had even asked around a bit among my classmates—some of them very talented—and learned that outside of a standard interview and a we'll-let-you-know, she hadn't offered any of the others employment, not even seniors and grad students. While vanity may be the sustaining shadow of every self, I knew that I was not so much better than everyone else that I warranted that much extra consideration.

. . . Unless, of course, the personal liking she had taken to me had caused Ann to build me up as some sort of Da Vinci to her employers. In which case, I knew that I would be very uncomfortable at Angra. I did not want an unfair advantage, and I did not want to be anyone's pet.

But Ann anticipated this reaction as she had so many others. The logic of it was compelling, and there was only one real way to handle it. The time had come for the truth.

It was a lovely day in late April, sunny and cool and crystal clear. The fresh green of spring still frothed across the land and the smells of the damp earth were heavy with life. I was again drinking coffee with Ann, only this time I had managed by judicious class-cutting to provide us with a three-day weekend together and we were taking coffee on the terrace of a place in the mountains which she had rented or Angra had owned or a friend had lent—I was never clear which—and I was wearing a maroon silk robe many sizes too small for me, with a golden, pop-eyed dragon coiling about itself upon the left breast, and I was peeling an orange and wondering how I was going to tell her that I didn't want the job just because she had taken a fancy to me, and if that wasn't it, what was?

"I suppose that we must discuss it sooner or later," she said before I gave voice to what I was thinking. "It is not your academically acquired abilities with computers in which Angra is most interested."

"Could you be more specific?" I said, still studying the orange peels.

"You have a unique mental *rapport* with computers."

"And if I do," I said, "how might you know of it?"

"*My* unique mental ability involves other people's minds."

"Telepathy? You can tell what I'm thinking?"

"Yes."

Oh, I tested her on a few strings of numbers and lines of poetry, but I believed her before she proved it. I guess it is not overly difficult for the possessor of a paranormal ability to believe that there might be others around.

"I didn't think it could be my sweet personality."

"But I am very fond of you," she responded, perhaps a trifle too quickly.

"Why is Angra hiring paranormals?" I asked. "And are there many others?"

"None like you," she said. "Any company with a group such as ours would have a terrific edge over the competition."

"It sounds somewhat like an unethical edge, even without hearing the particulars of what I'd be doing."

She rose to her feet and folded her arms. Her lip curled. I had never seen her angry before.

"Look around you," she said. "The country is going to hell in a handcart. The whole world is. Why? We have an energy crisis on our hands, that's why. It can be beaten. How? The technology is there—only pieces of it are tied up by dozens of different concerns. This one has a good lead in one sort of thing, that one in another. This one has an almost-good patent pending on something else, that one has a brilliant concept but no hardware yet. They're falling all over each other, blocking each other, getting in each other's ways. Supposing one company cut through all the crap, got its hands on everything good in the area right away and then pushed it into reality? Cheap, clean energy, and lots of it, that's what. No more crisis. A lot of toes would be stepped on. There would be a lot of lawsuits and maybe an antitrust action later. But so what? A company as big as Angra can roll with all that—

stall, settle, compromise. And the results? We *will* solve the energy crisis. We can do it within ten years. You want to watch them falling all over each other until we're on the brink of disaster, or are you willing to help do something about it? That's what Angra wants you for, that's why Angra wants your special talent. Are you going to help?"

I drank my coffee. I was glad that I finally had a straight story as to what I'd be doing, and that I still had a month in which to think about it.

In June I went to work for Angra, and Ann and I remained friendly. It was not until much later that we began to drift apart, as I felt increasingly that I was just an assignment for her. Circumstances sometimes seemed to indicate it, but I lacked her ability to know how someone really felt. This could have been a mistake on my part. She behaved coolly the first time that I went out with another woman, and later she presented me with a copy of Colette's *Cheri*. This was somewhere near the end of my tenure with Angra, but before the difficulties had arisen. I could not tell by reading that story of the young man who did not appreciate the older woman until it was too late whether it meant that she really liked me and was hurt by my behavior, or whether she was bothered by the fact that she was older than me. That's the trouble with literature. Ambiguity.

I could look about me now and see that, true to Ann's prediction, Angra had broken the energy crisis. Only, somewhere along the line, something had gone wrong. . .

"Damn!"

I stuffed my napkin and papers into the empty cup and tossed them into a nearby waste bin. I began walking about the campus then. There were several parking lots. Should I try stealing a car?

"Dr. Porter. About my grade. . ."

I turned suddenly. I hadn't heard him approach—a thin boy with a bad complexion and long brown hair. His mouth opened.

"I'm sorry," he said. "I thought you were my professor. . ."

"And you want your grade?"

"Yes, sir. I'll be leaving in a little while, and I thought—"

"Give me your name and section," I said. "Maybe I can help."

"James Martin Brown," he answered. "Political Science 106."

Tick. Tick. Terick.

"You were carrying a B," I told him. "You pulled a B on your final. Your grade should be a B."

His eyes widened. I smiled.

"I work in the office," I said. "Computer. Some of the stuff sticks."

He grinned.

"Thanks. I can sleep easy on the train home."

He turned and hurried off.

Train? I'd almost forgotten the tracks nearby. Some trains carried passengers, most carried freight and some were mixed. Most were fully automated now—those hauling freight exclusively so—though, unlike the trucks, they still had a few human troubleshooters aboard. The railroad union had held out longer than the Teamsters on this point. . .

I turned my attention once more toward the distant tracks.

I coiled . . . In, and back . . . Through, along. . .

There was a train due by in a little less than an hour. But it carried passengers. *Tick*. There was another in about three hours. Mixed. *Tickter*. One in about five hours. Freight. These last two were headed for Memphis. *Terick*.

I turned and began walking toward the tracks. There was a stand of trees farther to the west. I shifted my course in that direction. It seemed a good place to wait.

I had not hunted up the boy's grade out of pure altruism. If he were questioned later about strangers on campus, I wanted him thinking of me as someone who belonged, someone who had even done him a favor. No stranger.

I crossed the tracks and hiked on over to the trees. I located a sheltered place and sat down. Waiting there, amid shade and mosquitos, I ran back through the system and studied the manifest for that third run. There was to be a human crew of three aboard—engine, freight and caboose. Usually, I understood, they got together in a comfortable place and played cards. The trains were as safe as the trucks. This one was scheduled to haul twenty-two filled freight cars and three empty passenger cars for delivery in Memphis.

Where should I try to board? It depended on where the crew had located itself, a thing I hoped to discern when the unscheduled stop occurred. It would be nice to ride in one of the passenger cars, though.

It was too soon to program in the stop. Some overzealous employee could theoretically spot it if I fooled with the train's computer too far in advance. I sat listening to the birds and watching a few clouds rise in the east. I thought of possible courses of action I might take further along the line. I thought about Cora. . .

I felt the vibrations of the first train a long way off. I watched it when it finally roared by, and I listened to its rumbling fade again in the distance. I checked back and found that the others were still scheduled as they had been. For a second—just a bare second—as I did this, it seemed that I felt that shadowy presence once again, regarding me. I withdrew quickly and continued to brood upon the future.

After a time, I dozed. I was awakened by the approach of the second train. The sun had moved farther into the west. There was a certain stiffness in my knees and shoulders. My mouth had grown dry.

I stretched and cracked my joints and watched the other train pass. I checked once more after the freighter. On its way now, still on schedule, no changes. I programmed in the stop, using the nearest electrical mileage-marker as a guide. I wished that I had had the foresight to buy a few candy bars and a can of soda at the place back on campus. I chewed a blade of grass and tried to recall the last time I had ridden on a train.

When it did finally arrive it began to slow on schedule. There came a squealing noise as brakes were applied, and the ground shuddered. The engine drifted past me, slowing, slowing. Several cars went on by, still slowing, and finally the entire procession ground to a halt. It stood there in the long shadows, shuddering, while I readied myself for a dash.

I heard voices to my left. A man was climbing down from the caboose. Another followed him. The

second one turned to shout something to a third
person who remained aboard. The two on the
ground conferred for a time, then split up and
moved forward, passing along both sides of the
train.

I coiled into the computer. Someone was querying
it concerning the stop at the moment I entered into
it. The one who remained behind, I decided, was
checking the systems while the others looked for
some external cause for the halt.

The man on my side of the train peered between
the cars and looked beneath each one as he passed,
apparently determined to eyeball the situation all
the way up to the engine. I caused the doors of the
nearest passenger car to open, dashed across, entered and released them immediately.

There followed a long wait, as I wondered whether
I had been seen. My car was dark inside, as were the
other two. I crouched low in one of the seats and
stared out of the window. After a number of minutes
had passed, I breathed a little more easily. Still, it
was another good ten minutes before I heard the
crunch of gravel along the side to my right. I
crouched even lower and waited for it to pass. I
continued to wait. Shortly, the other passed on my
left.

· I sighed, and some of the tension went out of me. I
checked the computer again. I did not relax completely until a "Hold" order was removed and the
train gave a lurch. Slowly, we ground forward. The
motion grew more even, we began to pick up speed. I
sat up straight again.

When our speed grew uniform, I rose and inspected all three cars. I decided to locate myself in

the most forward one, so that I might hear the sounds of anyone approaching from the rear. I was not sure that I would be able to, over all of the other noises, but it made me feel a little safer.

Then I settled myself and clicked, ticked and de-ricked my way back into the central computer for the region, where I removed all memory of the train's unscheduled halt and replaced it with the simple fact that we were running late. I watched the correction order formulated and transmitted. I felt the train pick up speed as the adjustment was made. If no human observer had spotted the situation before I'd cleaned it up, I was relatively safe. I felt that I was learning to mask myself properly.

I watched the countryside roll past me. This far, this far now I had made it. I began to feel that I had a small chance.

"Cora, I'm coming," I said.

The wheels chuckled mechanically. The sun plunged toward another extinction, above my goal.

TWELVE

The telegraphic ragtime of the clicking wheels lulled me. I was not sleepy, having rested sufficiently while I awaited the train. But a kind of mental numbness came over me and my limbs felt heavy. It was a reaction, I suppose, to the furious pace of the past several days. Too many events, crowded too closely together. I had burned a lot of adrenalin, lived and relived a lot of trauma. I knew that there was more to come, but my mind rebelled at considering it. I just wanted to sit there, thinking of nothing, watching the dark countryside pass. For a long while, this is exactly what I did.

I had my hands clasped behind my head and my feet stretched out before me.

As to how much time had passed since I'd boarded, I was uncertain. I was for a time simply enjoying the great Taoist principle of *wu wei*—doing nothing—when suddenly I was in a garden. It seemed an awkward time for Enlightenment to have been thrust suddenly upon me, and so I was immediately wary.

There were vivid images of flowers all about me and a mixture of their fragrances came strongly to me. Despite my wariness I was, for several moments, overwhelmed. It was a senses-assaulting floral chaos.

"Ann?" I said, seeking stability. "What is it this time?"

But there was nothing more—only the maddening riot of colors and aromas, changing now as if a bizarre kaleidoscope were being slowly turned.

Then a voiceless note of fear burst forth, filling my brain. I felt Ann's presence behind it, though it seemed as if only a part of her attention were turned in my direction.

"Ann?"

"Yes. Troubles," I seemed to hear her say, and then there was a vague sensation of pain.

Abruptly, the flowers began to fade, the aromas grew more delicate. . .

". . . Hurts. There! Stopped him!"

"Ann! What the hell's going on?"

"He's here . . . Willy Boy's come for me."

And then there was a rearrangement of my senses. I was with her, in a way we had shared only a few times in the past. I found myself a guest within her mind, looking out through her eyes, listening with her ears, feeling her physical distress. . .

We were in an apartment, a fairly large one. I had no idea where it was located. Peripheral vision showed me that it was elegantly furnished, but our gaze was fixed upon Willy Boy, who leaned against the wall in an entranceway, a wide living room away from us. He was slightly hunched and breathing heavily. A half-wall separated us from what seemed to be a small kitchen area. To the right, a large window looked out upon a brightly lit skyline I could not identify—though I felt it was somewhere in the East. Off in the distance was her computer-cum-telephone-etcetera, or "home unit" as almost everyone called them these days. We stood before a light brown leather sofa, leaning upon a Moroccan table. There was a pain in our chest, but we were giving as well as receiving.

"Sister, I can see your point," Willy Boy was saying, "but you're only delayin' things, that's all."

Ann threw more force into the hallucination she was creating for him. She was causing him to experience violent chest pains, apparently as real-seeming to him as the actual ones he had commenced within her. He seemed to find it very distracting. He had just let up on his own efforts, giving her a few moments to go looking for me, to bring me to her.

"A weapon, Ann! That heavy ashtray, the lamp—anything! Brain him!" I said. "Switch to the physical. Knock him out. It'll stop him. Push your advantage!"

"I—can't," she told me. "It's taking everything I've got to hold him. . ."

"Then go kick him in the balls! Jab those long fingernails into his eyes! He'll kill you if you don't take him out!"

"I know," she said. "But if I get any nearer the advantage will be his. The closer you get, the greater his strength."

"Do you have a gun?"

"No."

"Can you get to the kitchen and get a knife?"

"He's closer to the kitchen than I am. It's no good."

I had distracted her. I felt a burning within her chest, a pain in the arm—similar to that which I had experienced at the terminal. She projected a full-scale image of it back upon him, and he raised his hand to press his palm against his own chest.

"I think he has a real heart condition," she said. "I can play on his fear and muddy his mind."

"For how long?"

"I don't know."

I searched frantically for a way to help her. In a sudden rush I remembered how much I had once cared for her.

"Your phone number—what is it?"

As it occurred within her mind, Willy Boy pushed himself away from the wall and took several steps toward her. She hit him again and he sagged.

"You can't save me," she said. "That is not why I reached for you."

"We have to fight," I told her. "I'm going to try."

"I know that. But he is too strong. It is only a matter of time. I want something you showed me earlier. Something stronger than my flowers—a world that is cold and metal and filled with electricity and logic. I want to embrace the machines, and only you can take me to them."

"Follow me," I said, even as Matthews began to straighten once more.

Derick. Tick. Cantaterclick.

For a moment, the Coil Effect seemed to merge with the rhythms of the train, and I was dimly aware of a new-risen moon touching the fields beyond the glass to a pearly texture as I wound my way into the train's computer and plunged through the linkages that followed the track, back, back to the regional control center, back. . .

Clack.

I raced through a spreading map of the territory, looking for incoming and outgoing routes. . .

Telephone line hookups were what I was after. I just had to find the right one, had to get into the telephone system itself. . .

Ann was with me, too dazed to protest, if she wished to, at the blinding speed, the bewildering sensations, as I sped through a number of false starts, up blind alleys and back, moving at a pace I had never before essayed, until I located what I was looking for.

Even as I did this, I became aware of the recurrence of her chest pains. Willy Boy wasn't losing any time at all.

. . . An infinity of bright bees burned all about me, analogue to all the dial tones. They winked into and out of existence—virtual bees—and within the clacking and buzzing my mind supplied the ringing, the chiming, of multitudes of bells. . .

I located and activated the mechanism for placing a call. Her number, I learned as I tripped the relay, was in Ridgewood, New Jersey. In the instant between my activation of the circuit and the actual ringing of her unit, between her pain, the swaying train and the image of Willy Boy advancing, I became aware of the observer. That silent, dark presence I had sensed in the past was with us again, drawing nearer, watching. . .

The unit rang. It distracted the lumbering ex-preacher. Matthews stopped and glanced at it, looked back at Ann. She was breathing heavily and perspiring now, bent forward, one hand still upon the table, supporting herself, the other pressed against her chest. The ache and the tightness had begun to ebb by the fourth ring, though she was too occupied with the pain and the present focus of her attention to reassert her earlier illusion.

It rang again. How many had she set the damned thing for, anyway?

On the sixth ring her computer answered it with a recording and offered to take a message. As soon as that occurred, I was able to find my way into the computer and to take stock of the things it controlled.

Willy Boy turned suddenly at a noise from the kitchen. It was only the automatic toaster setting itself, breadless, to work. He strode back in that direction and looked around the corner.

"Run, Ann!" I told her. "Try to get out the door!"

"Too weak, Steve," she said. "I'd fall on my face."

"Try!"

She let go the table and swayed. I felt her dizziness. She collapsed upon the sofa.

"Take a deep breath and try again."

She began to comply, but Matthews was already turning back.

"Why is he doing this to you?" I asked.

The buzzer on the microwave stove filled the air with a nasty, insistent sound.

Willy Boy turned again, apparently unable to concentrate, and entered the kitchen.

"I didn't tell The Boss that you were still alive," she said. "But he found out from the wreck, decided he couldn't trust me any more. I could see in his mind that he was afraid I might—take your side. Decided not to give me the chance . . . God! what a beautiful world the network is! I'd rather read machines than people. I wish I'd been born with your power instead—"

The buzzing stopped.

"Sister, I don't know how you managed that," Matthews said, entering from the kitchen. "But you're only prolongin'—"

I turned off all the lights. I heard him curse.

"Try to pull yourself together enough to make a run for it," I said.

The lights were on dimmers. I began cycling them on and off rapidly, producing a strobe effect. Matthews' movements seemed almost comically jerky as he threw up an arm, covered his eyes, then tried shading them. He took a step forward and halted.

Then his expression changed. He placed the heels of his hands over his eyes, blocking out all light. I felt the sharp, terrible pain which ran through Ann's body. She uttered a short cry. For a moment, we almost lost touch.

. . . And somewhere, still near, I felt the half-familiar presence of the silent one.

Willy Boy took another step forward, another, his power growing as the distance narrowed.

The television set came to life as I activated the control.

Willy Boy kept coming. The pain grew, spread. . . .

I increased the volume and began flipping from channel to channel. In some areas they have an around-the-clock—

Yes!

"—glorious day!"

Matthews froze. He lowered his hands. I let the lighting return to normal.

"—in Jesus' words, 'Blessed be the. . .' "

Willy Boy turned bright red. His eyes grew very wide. Again the pain was eased. He stared at the impeccably garbed man with the upraised hand and the ingratiating smile.

"Son of a bitch!" he said. He looked wildly at Ann, speaking suddenly as if she were not his victim of the moment. "The damned reporters crucified me! They should get him! I trained that oily Bible-thumper! Kicked him out, too! When his hand wasn't in the collection basket it was in some choirboy's pants! Worthless little whelp!" He gestured toward the set. "Did they ever go after him, though? No. I could have had him up on charges. Did a Christian thing and let him go. I was already in trouble myself. Didn't make that much difference then. Figured they'd get him sooner or later, anyhow. Look at him now, though! Listen to him! They never did. There's no justice. Hunger and thirst after righteousness and you'll wind up on Maalox!"

He rushed up to the set and slammed the button which turned it off. He began to rub his forehead then.

I turned the set back on again, full blast.

"Let us pray—"

"Damn it!" he cried, turning it off again.

I turned it back on.

". . . Thy kingdom come—"

He hit the button, and I did it again.

". . . on earth as it is in heaven. . ."

He tried holding it in the Off position then. I overrode him.

". . . and forgive us our trespasses. . ."

He made a loud, bleating, animal noise and dropped to his knees. He crawled forward, reaching, located the plug and pulled at it ". . . not into temptation. . ."

He was shaking when he rose, breathing heavily. I began strobing the lights again. I set the stove to buzzing once more. I kicked on the computer's taped greeting. None of these seemed to reach him this time, though. He rushed forward, set his teeth and glared down at Ann.

The pain became excruciating, and then a wave of blackness seemed to roll up through her. I drew her to me and held her as tightly as possible, as if I could somehow keep her alive within my own consciousness.

I knew that her body had died. But she seemed still to be with me.

"Ann?" I said, as I moved back through telephone exchanges.

"Yes?"

I linked with the regional unit, found an area where the traffic was slow.

"We lost," I said.

"I knew that we would. I told you."

. . . *The prospect swirled, racing beads on an infinite abacus. . .*

"I'm sorry. I tried."

"I know, Steve. Thank you. If I'd met you sooner
. . . I was always weak. I wish—"

The strange presence was suddenly nearer than it
had ever been before, almost palpable, something I
seemed just about ready to identify. . .

"Of course," she said, and I did not understand.
She was weak, growing weaker. She had no right to
exist at all now, except by this kind of symbiosis. I
did not know what I was going to do with her. "Let
me go now, Steve."

The presence grew stronger. It was almost intimidating. I held her more tightly, trying to share
my strength with her.

"It's all right," she said.

In that moment, I felt that it was, as if she had just
been granted some special vision I did not share.

"Really. I must go."

She began disengaging herself from my mental
grip.

"It is the big Angra research facility—Number
Four—just outside Carlsbad. That's what you want.
She's there," she said. "Good luck."

"Ann. . ."

The sensation, whatever it was, was like a parting
kiss. Then she moved toward the stranger, who welcomed her.

I had a vision of them, passing across a sheet-
metal plain where roses of aluminum, copper, brass
and tin swayed in an ozone breeze beneath a sky lit
by an arc of blue sparklight. The figure whose hand
she took wore a metal mask, unless of course that
was its face. . .

. . . I followed the track, back, back, to the
clackety-clack, to the ragtime rhythms, quad-

rupedante putrem sonitu quatit ungula campum, as we rocked, racing, westward, under the Southern moon full-risen, moonlight, night flight, seeming dreaming, track away. Steve, did she say?

   Clack.

THIRTEEN

I dozed after a time, a light and troubled sleep. Half-consciously, I checked periodically with the computer, keeping track of our distance from Memphis. I believe that I dreamed, but the particulars escaped me. I welcomed the distancing effect that a period of unconsciousness would place between me and the evening's events. Light and broken though it was, my slumber gave this much to me.

The moon had climbed much higher by the time I came fully awake and decided that I could no longer postpone full fore-thought. I did not want to take the chance of riding all of the way into the railroad yard. Which meant that another unscheduled stop was in order. I was not familiar with Memphis. I did not want to stop too far out of town and simply find myself lost in the middle of the night; and I did not relish the idea of a long walk through unfamiliar territory. I decided on a sudden stop right before the

railroad yard, unless something better presented
itself along the way.

While I had cleaned up the computer record of this
trip so far—back at regional—there was nothing I
would be able to do about the memory of two unexplained stops in the minds of the train's crew. The
stops would be reported and there would have to be
some sort of investigation. When it was seen that the
crew's story did not match the record, someone at
Angra who must now be hunting transportation
anomalies in this direction would be alerted. This
coming situation was the necessary result of my
present security. It was another reason for my getting off at a late point and not dawdling in the area. I
would have to move on as quickly as possible. I
began to wonder whether there were any way in
which I might provide a false trail for Angra's inves-
tigators. I began to consider what little I did know of
the geography of the area and to speculate as to what
might be quickly available to me.

So, later, when I initiated the braking program,
there were all sorts of lights in sight. I crouched
before the door, caused it to open and hit the ground
before we had come to a complete halt. I headed
forward, not wanting the crew to catch sight of me,
down off the siding and across a field. I did nothing
to the computer this time, other than to order it to
shut the door a little later.

When I felt comfortably out of sight I slowed to a
walk and caught my breath. I headed toward a row
of streetlights beyond darkened houses, crossed
some sort of drainage ditch and passed through
someone's yard. A dog began barking within the
house. It shut up after I made it to the sidewalk and
crossed the street.

I walked for about fifteen minutes after that, trying without success to get an idea as to where I was in relation to anything that might be of use to me. It was unfortunate that I had jumped off near a residential area. They are simply too dead after a certain hour to be of much use for the sorts of things I had in mind. I kept my mental ears open for the familiar voices of computers, but the only ones I could hear at all were too somnolent in terms of current activity to be kicked into service, most of them functioning as glorified timers at the moment.

I continued, turning after a time onto a larger thoroughfare. An occasional car passed, but I dismissed the notion of trying to flag one down. I did not want to leave anyone with the memory and possible description of a hitchhiker around this place at this time. I stretched my faculties as far as I could reach, casting about in all directions, seeking computer activity.

Faintly, far off to the right, there seemed to be some action. I turned right at the next corner and headed toward it. I kept walking past houses—darkened, for the most part—expecting to hit a commercial area. But I didn't.

Instead, the area remained unchanged but the signal grew stronger, finally reaching the point where I could read it clearly. It was some insomniac gamester engaged in an elaborate four-way contest involving two players in Mississippi and one in Kentucky. There was a light behind drawn curtains in a house across the street, up ahead, which might well be its source. I slowed my pace.

Lickticktertick.

. . . *I passed along the connections without disturbing their play. It was a telephone-line hookup, and the*

first exchange I got to I departed their circuit. Slowly
shifting holes in an enormous piece of luminous Swiss
cheese. . .

I plunged into, out of, along and through a great
number of these. I finally got the feeling, jumping from
circuit to circuit, for the ones which led to functioning
computers as opposed to those in use between people's
phones. . .

After three bad leads, I found my way into the Police
Department's main computer. There were security
wards, but after my bout with Big Mac I was able to
pass through these without slowing down. It was not
really the police computer that I had set out to locate,
however. Any of a number of others would have done
as well. All that I actually wanted was a detailed map of
the city. . .

I studied it for a long while, fixing in my memory the
features that I thought I could use. Next, I memorized a
few major thoroughfares—east-west and north-
south—so that when I finally hit one I would be into a
coordinate system. . .

I was about to disengage from the unit when it
occurred to me to seek myself within it.

Ricktatack. Backadaback. . .

. . . Donald BelPatri—[description and photo repro
code]. Armed and dangerous. Fugitive warrant,
Philadelphia. Theft, Angra Corp. Attempted homicide,
William Matthews. Auto theft. . .

I erased it. No sense in leaving things easy for them
when the opportunity to meddle is handy.

Still, I'd a feeling I would be back into the machine
pretty soon, once my nemesis at Angra got wind of the
railroad report. Running that thing down and trying to
erase it could take me all night, time I couldn't spare.

Besides, by now it was probably already in the system at Angra. In fact : . . . Maybe I had impulsively just provided them with another clue by wiping my record. Well . . . shit. Too late now. Think first next time. . .

Rackadack.

I found myself leaning against a tree. I only dimly recalled having halted. I began walking again, reviewing the street map, trying to fix it more firmly in mind.

Several blocks passed. Small streets. Nothing I was looking for. But up ahead. . .

An apartment complex, with a big parking lot.

I studied the place for long minutes, to see whether I could spot a guard of any sort, but I couldn't.

I could not start any of those cars mentally, I knew, not when they were cold like that. I needed a little juice in a machine's circuits to play around with.

However. . .

I entered the lot and began a long, slow stroll. The lighting was not always good, and if anyone saw me I knew that I must look suspicious, peering into car windows that way. Statistically, it just seemed possible that out of all those cars someone might have left the keys in one.

Twenty minutes later, I was beginning to doubt this, right before I located one—a black coupe, electric. I got in quickly, started it, backed it out of the parking place and got out of the lot fast. I didn't breathe easily until I had gone several miles.

I was onto a fairly wide street, which finally took me into a business district. I determined to follow it until I hit one of my coordinates or ten miles, whichever came first. In the later case, I would then turn around and follow it in the other direction backtracking and passing on until I hit one.

I came upon one fairly quickly, however, and turned onto it. Just a couple of miles, after that, I intersected with another. At last I knew where I was.

My mental map now oriented, I headed in the direction of the feature I sought. When the police car came up behind me I almost did something foolish. But prudence ruled and I halted at the stop light rather than flooring it and crashing through. When the light changed, the car passed me and shortly thereafter turned off to the left. I found myself shaking, though I knew that I should have felt a bit secure in the knowledge that there was nothing out on the car yet. I drove very carefully after that.

I saw an open diner. It wasn't on my schedule, but my stomach felt otherwise about it. I could see that the place was nearly deserted. I pulled into the lot, went in and had a club sandwich, a piece of pie and a cup of coffee. I washed up and repaired myself in the rest room, wishing I had a razor as I ran my hand over my now-stubbly chin. I took out my wallet and counted the bills. I generally carry a good amount of cash when I travel—I'm old-fashioned that way. I was pleased to see that I still had several hundred dollars. Good. That would be of help.

Driving again, and feeling much better, I continued along the rough route I had in mind, still wincing whenever I heard a siren.

While I did not know exactly where the place was, I hoped to come across signs as soon as I got into the vicinity. The city thinned out as I drove. Malls and building clusters came and went, and then there were only houses, farther and farther apart. Finally, a sign appeared, and I turned where it indicated.

A light plane came out of the north, circled and descended toward a bright area up ahead, my destination.

I slowed as I approached, locating the entrance drive and turning up it. The place did not seem exceptionally large or busy. It was just one of many small air transport services.

I found a spot in the uncrowded parking lot, turned off the engine, turned off the lights. I coiled then into the computer in the operations building which lay ahead and to my left. I flashed past the flights in progress information and the weather reports. There were eight 'copters on the ground, I learned. Two of them were being serviced and two had just come in recently and had not yet been gone over. Four were out on pads, fully serviced, fully fueled, awaiting use.

I studied what I could see of the field, trying to match eyeball with electronic information. The farthest one, of course, would be mine. . .

I left the keys in the car, the car in the lot, my footsteps on the lawn, bearing me far to the left, past the building on what appeared to be its blindest side. I kept to the shadows as much as possible, passing along behind a row of small hangars. Someone was in the first one, servicing a light plane.

Emerging near the pad I sought, I simply walked across fifteen meters of concrete and climbed into the pilot's seat in the vehicle I had chosen. There had been no outcry. If anybody had noticed me, perhaps they'd thought I'd some business there. I don't know.

I studied the controls. I had only the vaguest idea of what did what for anything. Still, there ought to be some simple switches for ignition or battery, something that would get some juice into the system.

I strapped myself in and experimented. After half a minute of fumbling, I got the engine to kick over. Simultaneously, the flight computer came to life. I was still vividly fresh on helicopter computers and automatic pilots.

I activated the takeoff program. The sound of the engine increased in intensity and the blades made a bullroaring noise overhead. I followed the operations of the various systems. Everything appeared to be in order.

As I rose, I wondered whether I should have any lights on on the vehicle. I decided against it. Why make things any easier for anyone else, just for a little safety? Of course, they would doubtless try tracking me on their radar, but I intended to get very low very shortly for what I had in mind, and I had hopes of losing them—at least for awhile.

I didn't cross the field. I headed away from it to the left, constantly scanning the sky for anything incoming, until I felt safely out of range of the place.

And then, to the northwest. I preferred skirting the town to flying over it. I kept low as we passed above fields and farms, but high enough to avoid power lines as we chased the falling moon. Finally, the ground began to drop away, gently, and a little later I was given a view of the dark, star-shot river. Again, I reviewed the police map as I drove on toward it, and when I finally came to its bank and passed on out over the water I turned to the left and headed downriver.

There was an empty stretch of road about a mile from the place which I hoped would satisfy my needs. I set it down there, climbing out quickly, got out of the way and sent it aloft again. Having checked out a variety of pre-planned flight programs it possessed, I directed it to fly to Oklahoma City, maintaining a low altitude for the first twenty miles and then following its normal programming for the balance of the trip.

I turned to my left and began walking. I came to a section composed mainly of warehouses, just a few small lights about them, watchmen doubtless around somewhere, not that it mattered. Moving on past, I enjoyed the smells from the river, from which a light, warm, humid breeze was coming. Tomorrow would probably be hot and muggy, but the night was pleasant. There were no city sounds here, only insects in the grasses beside the road. And so far, no traffic along it.

I took my time, not wanting my arrival to coincide too closely with the passage of the 'copter. I followed a curve in the road which took me around a warehouse and nearer to the water.

The next big view to open up included people. There were overhead lights playing down upon a docking area, and I could now hear the creaking of a winch. A boom was swinging. A number of barges, anchored in various positions, came into sight. The one at the wharf was being loaded with large flats of cartons, which a pair of workers moved to strap into place once they were deposited. I found myself a comfortable and unobtrusive spot on the bank above the road's right shoulder, and I settled there to observe the enterprise for a time. There were still quite a few flats waiting upon the pier for loading.

. . . A quick tick derick flick through the barge's computer, which was now functioning in order to compare the manifest and what actually came aboard, told me a number of interesting things: the vessel would be departing in about two hours, and it would be stopping in Vicksburg.

No hurry then, and I could think of several arguments against prematurity in my approach. So I watched the operation and counted heads and checked out things which occurred to me with the computer.

There were the two men aboard the barge, loading the cargo into place. I assumed the crane itself to have a human operator, though it occurred to me that the large, red-haired man, wearing faded jeans and a blue and white striped sweater, who was seated atop a packing crate drinking a cup of coffee, might be manipulating it remotely by means of the small device near his right hand, which he occasionally raised.

Tick-terick.

No. He was just calling off inventory items through a broadcast unit. There was someone in the shed manipulating the crane. Another man was sprawled—sleeping or drunk or both—upon the decking, his back against the shack, head rolled to the side upon his shoulder, mouth open, eyes closed.

I guessed that the big man on the crate was the one listed in the vessel's computer as "Ship's master: C. Catlum". The computer itself was similar to that on my houseboat, and I read that its standing orders required two live hands while the barge was adrift. I assumed that the guy propped up against the shed qualified loosely as the other one. I further assumed that some sort of union rules required that the vessel

be loaded and unloaded by someone other than its
captain and crew. I noted three cars and a truck
parked in a lot behind the shed. The cars probably
belonged to the laborers, the truck to the warehous-
ing company which had stored the cargo. I strained
and made out the lettering "Deller Storage" on its
side. Good. It seemed I had a reasonable picture of
the situation now. I cast about then for the best
approach. There was just no way I could sneak
aboard—I had discarded that notion long ago.

I watched for over an hour, assuring myself that
there was no one else around. The stack of flats grew
lower and lower. Another fifteen minutes, I decided. . .

When that time had passed, I rose to my feet and
made my way slowly down toward the lighted area.
There wasn't much left to stow now. I walked out
across the planks and up to the side of the packing
case. The man propped against the shed still hadn't
moved.

"And hello to you, too," said the man on the case,
not looking in my direction.

"Captain Catlum?" I said.

"You're one up on me."

"Steve," I said, "Lanning. I understand you'll be
leaving for Vicksburg in a little while."

"I won't deny it," he said.

"I'd like a ride down that way."

"I'm not running a taxi service."

"Didn't figure you were. But when I mentioned to
the man at Deller Storage that I'd always wanted to
ride on one of these, he said maybe I should see you."

"Deller's been out of business two years now. They
should take that name off the trucks."

"Whatever they call it these days, he said if I could

pay my way I could probably get a ride."

"The regulations say no."

"He said maybe fifty dollars. What do you say?"

Catlum looked at me for the first time and he smiled, a very engaging thing. He was a ruggedly good-looking guy; about my own age, I guessed.

"Why, I didn't write the regulations. Some fellow in an office back East prob'ly did."

The crane swung back and descended. It caught hold of another flat and raised it.

"You realize, I'd be jeopardizing my career by taking you aboard," he said.

"He really said a hundred dollars. I suppose I could manage that."

He did something to the machine at his side, indicating the loading of that last flat.

"You like to play checkers?" he asked.

"Well—yes," I said.

"Good. My partner's going to be out for a while. What'd you say was the name of that man you talked to?"

"Wilson, or something like that."

"Oh, yeah. Why'd you wait so long before you came on down?"

"I saw you were busier at first."

He grinned and nodded. Then he came down from the crate, leaned forward and counted the remaining flats. He reached out and entered something into the unit. I was suddenly awed. There had been no real way of telling while he was seated, and he was well-enough proportioned that it was almost difficult to believe, but the man was about seven feet tall.

"Okay," he said, hooking the unit onto his belt and

handing me his cup and a huge thermos jug. "Take these, will you?"

Then he leaned forward and scooped up the unconscious man. He draped him over his left shoulder and headed up the gangway as if the extra weight meant nothing. He headed into the small cabin and dumped him onto a bunk. Then he turned toward me and took his cup and thermos.

"Thanks," he said, hanging the cup on a hook and depositing the jug in a corner.

I was reaching for my wallet, but he walked away, departing the cabin, and checked on the rest of the incoming cargo. When this was done he turned to me, grinning again.

"Say, I'm going to have to break the shoreside computer hookup in a few minutes," he said. "Do you think Wilson might have left a message about you in the company machine?"

I shrugged.

"I don't know. He didn't say."

"You a sporting man, Steve?"

"Sometimes."

"I'll bet you a hundred dollars he didn't say a word. You know old Wilson—or whoever."

I figured I could probably use the money, and I wanted to strengthen my story, as he obviously believed I was lying—though I didn't think it really mattered that much to him.

"You're on," I said, and I coiled.

"Okay. They'll finish stowing the stuff in another five minutes. Let's go and see now."

I accompanied him back to the cabin, where he approached a terminal and punched an inquiry after messages in the warehouse computer.

STEVE LANNING WILL BE ALONG, the screen flashed.

"I'll be damned," he said. "Old Wilson remembered. That's a fine trick. Looks as if you ride free. Well, we'd better be gettin' ready to cast off now. Say, how good a checkers player are you?"

No sense in putting myself down. Besides, I was pretty good.

"Not bad," I said.

"Good. Let's make it two dollars a game. I think there's time for fifty quick ones before breakfast."

I didn't think it possible that anyone could beat me fifty straight games of checkers. Catlum won the first dozen games so fast that my head spun. He never paused. He just moved whenever his turn came. Then he poured us each a cup of coffee and we took them outside while his companion snored.

We looked out over the waters and I thought of Mark Twain and of all the things that had come down the river over the years.

"You running from something?" he asked.

"Running to something," I answered.

"Well, good luck to you," he said.

"Don't you get bored pushing a barge?" I asked.

"Haven't done it in a long time," he said. "This is a sentimental journey."

"Oh." I was silent for awhile. Then, "This must really have been something when it was all wild," I observed.

He nodded.

"Pretty. Of course, the last time I came down this way I wound up in jail."

We watched until our cups were empty and then we went back inside. He beat me another dozen games, and then a false dawn occurred in the east. I bore down, I played as well as I could, but he just kept winning. He chuckled each time, taking my two dollars or making change for me. I finally decided that he had to be taken down a peg. I coiled into the computer and installed the tightest impromptu game program I could come up with—which I guess was only as good as the programmer, because I leaned heavily on it for a time and he kept right on winning.

He got his hundred dollars sometime late that morning, and then I had to sack out on the other bunk while he went out to look at the cargo.

I don't know how long I had been asleep when I dreamed my way through a Coil Effect. I was inside that 'copter again, skimming across the countryside, when suddenly I was flanked by a pair of heavier-looking machines. They opened fire without preamble, tearing my vehicle to bits. I remained within the computer's shrinking sensorium as it plunged earthward. Then came the impact and I awakened briefly. I knew that it had been more than a dream. The feelings accompanying the phenomenon were second nature, and the ones I'd just experienced had been real.

But there was nothing to do at this point and my eyes were still heavy. I drifted back to sleep. I dreamed more dreams, but they were garden-variety and fugitive.

What finally slowly brought me around later was a moaning sound—repeated, drawn-out. I opened my eyes. The cabin was dark. The fellow on the other bunk was making the noises. For a minute, I was disoriented, and then I realized where I was.

I sat up on the edge of the bunk and massaged my

brow. Had I really slept away most of the day? My body must have needed the rest badly, to put me out like that. I looked over at the other bunk. The man who tossed there, arm across his face, appeared to be in the throes of a horrible hangover. As this did not make him the best of company, I rose and turned toward the doorway, realizing as I did that I was ravenously hungry. I also wanted a bathroom.

I passed outside. Catlum was leaning against the bulkhead, grinning at me.

"Just about time to go, Steve," he said. "I was going to get you up in a few more minutes."

I cast about in all directions. I did not see anything that lived up to my expectation of Vicksburg. I told him so.

"Well, you've got a good point there," he said. "Vicksburg's still a little ways downstream. But we're already long past Transylvania. Most important of all, though, the captain's waking up."

"Wait a minute. Aren't you Captain Catlum?"

"Indeed I am," he answered. "Only I'm not captain of this particular vessel—one of those little fine points they sometimes get touchy about."

"But when I saw you supervising the loading—"

"—I was doin' a little favor for a friend who couldn't say no to free drinks."

"But what about the other guy? Aren't there supposed to be two people aboard?"

"Alas! That other gentleman was taken out in a fist fight. It comes of drinking and carousing. He was in no shape to make the trip. Now, up forward there—"

"Hold on! It sounds as if you stole this vessel!"

"Lord, no! I've probably just saved that poor

man's job." He jerked a massive thumb back toward the cabin. "I've no desire to embarrass him by waiting around for his thanks, though. Now, we'd better be jumpin' in a few minutes. The water'll be shallow off to port, near that promontory. We can just wade ashore."

Wading, I reflected, tends to be easier when one is seven feet tall. But I said, "Why'd you do it?"

"I needed a ride to Vicksburg, too."

I was about to say that the computer had him listed as captain, but how was I to know that? Instead, I said, "I'm going to hit the head first."

"I'll be gettin' my gear while you do that thing."

While I did that thing I also coiled into the computer and checked again. "Ship's master: David G. Holland" I read. So Catlum had fudged the records, too, temporarily—just an observation, as I could hardly afford a holier-than-thou attitude on that count. But knowing my story about a Wilson at Deller's referring me to him to be a complete fabrication, he must have been puzzled about how I did know his name and how I'd gotten my message into the computer. On the other hand, he didn't seem to care and he hardly seemed the sort to go running to authorities about a fugitive. He might even be one himself. I decided that it was safe to accompany him ashore at the point he had indicated.

When the time came, we jumped. He did wade. I swam. My teeth were chattering when we finally reached the strand, but Catlum set up a brisk pace which was eventually warming.

"Where are we headed?" I finally asked him.

"Oh, a couple of more miles along the road here there's a little eatery I know," he said.

My stomach growled in reply.

". . . Then a little further on there's a small town with just about anything you'd want. Maybe even a new pair of pants."

I nodded. My garments were even shabbier now. I was starting to look like a bum. He slapped me on the shoulder then and increased his pace. I forced myself to match it. I thought about the barge and its hungover captain, winding along the river up ahead. I had to acknowledge that if anyone somehow traced me to the barge the trail was going to be even more confused than I'd originally intended. I owed this oversized con man that much.

When we got to the restaurant I was almost dizzy with hunger. We settled at a table off to the side and I ordered a steak. My companion did what I'd only fantasized. He ordered three. He finished them, too, and started in on several pieces of pie while I was still working on mine. He called for coffee so often that the waitress left a pot on the table.

Finally, he sighed and looked at me and said, "You know, you could use a shave."

I nodded.

"Didn't bring my barber along," I said.

"Wait a minute." He leaned to the side and opened his duffle bag. He rummaged in it for several moments, then withdrew one of those plastic disposable razors and a small tube of shaving cream. He pushed them across the table toward me. "I always carry a couple of these for emergencies. You look like one."

He poured himself another cup of coffee.

"Thanks," I said, spearing the last edible morsel on my plate and glancing back toward the Men's Room. "I'll take you up on it."

I went back and washed, lathered my face, shaved and combed my hair. The image which regarded me from the mirror actually looked presentable, well-nourished and rested then. Amazing. I disposed of the disposable and departed the facility.

Our table was empty, save for the bill.

After a moment I had to laugh, for the first time in a long while. I couldn't hold it against him. I should have seen that one coming. I shook my head, feeling something vaguely like a loss other than my money.

That Catlum was sure one hell of a checkers player.

FOURTEEN

Moving off. The skin of the sky was very blue and the song of the air whistled inside my helmet around my ears. I gripped the handlebars and maintained a steady pace within my lane. The 'cycle held the road beautifully.

I had found the little town right where Catlum had said it would be, up the road, and I had indeed purchased new trousers there—also a shirt and a jacket. Except for a few stores, though, I was stymied. They had a vehicle rental place, but it was closed and I couldn't locate the owner or manager. Upon reflection, this may have been just as well. It resulted in my getting in some good thinking time.

I had passed a little motel on my way into town. I could get a room, and the shower itself would be worth it. I was not sleepy after the day's hibernation, but I wanted to be out of sight while I waited and I did not feel like skulking about the countryside.

When I said cash and he saw that I had no luggage, the clerk asked for payment in advance. But that was okay. I gave him a false name and out-of-state address, of course, got the room, cleaned myself up and stretched out on the bed.

Still feeling alert, I reviewed everything that had happened—from the Keys to Baghdad and on along my current odyssey to the present moment. I thought about Cora. I knew where she was now, and I felt that she was safe for the time being. A dead hostage is after all no hostage, and they would derive no benefit from making her suffer until or unless I could be made to watch. While recent experiences demonstrated the fineness of the distinction, I felt that Barbeau would still actually rather have me alive and working for him again than dead. This much of what he had said back in Philadelphia, I believed. If this could not be, however, he wanted me dead. What he feared most, I was certain, was probably my going to the Justice Department with my story. I could see myself at a hearing, playing computer tricks to demonstrate what I was saying. No. He would not like that. And so long as he had a live Cora for insurance, he knew that this would not come to pass. He would hang onto a live Cora now until he had a dead BelPatri—for he must realize by now that I wasn't coming back.

I had remained safe so far by exploiting the new, manipulative aspect of my paranormal ability. Barbeau had not been prepared for anything like it, and I was certain it had him worried. I realized, too, that I was going to have to rely upon it from here on out, to exploit it fully, for offense and defense, for the rest of my journey, to keep him off balance, to maintain an edge.

I intended renting a vehicle on the morrow, for the next stage of my journey. As I had just been reminded at the desk, however, one either charges or pays cash for things—and my funds were dwindling and my credit cards all said DONALD BELPATRI.

No problem, I decided, remembering the policeman with the little box, back in Philadelphia. No matter what the card says, I can alter what the machine says it reads there.

But wait . . . It was not quite that simple.

For one thing, altering the account number signal would not be sufficient. It had to be altered to something intelligible and acceptable. Otherwise, the transmitter would receive a notice that there was something wrong, and I would be in trouble.

For another thing, the cards all bore my name. While this meant nothing to the computer, which was only interested in an account number associated with some name on file, a human operator on this end would see the name and would also doubtless create a local, personal record of the transaction. This was unacceptable, with Angra shaking the shrubbery after me.

I studied one of my credit cards. The name and numbers were embossed in such a fashion that I couldn't really do much to alter their values. With the point of my pocket knife, though, it seemed that I might be able to scrape a letter off flush with the surface of the card, so that it would not print onto any paper inserts. A little scribbling and smudging could then mask the letter-sized gap. . .

I got rid of the B and the RI.

DONALD ELPAT. It looked good enough. They never seem to look at the card itself, anyhow, except to check whether it's still valid and sometimes to see that it's signed.

I studied my signature on the reverse side of the card: my usual half-legible scrawl. Excellent. I added a few more squiggles and no one could say that it didn't read DONALD ELPAT there, too.

. . . And while I did this, I composed a series of simple biographical data concerning my new persona.

That done, I turned my attention to the matter of accounts. Certain numbers simply would not work. If I altered the signal from the Elpat card to a number in a series that was not in use the receiving computer would take immediate exception. If I chose one corresponding to a real account that had something wrong with it—non-payment by the real owner or such—I would also find myself without credit.

I thought about accounts.

Good old 078-05-1120 occurred to me immediately. Back in the 30's, when the Social Security Act was passed and the first cards issued, a wallet manufacturer had decided to insert a facsimile of one in the little Celluloid-covered pocket of his product, to demonstrate its use to the unimaginative. It did not occur to him that, for the sake of consistency in his estimation of human intelligence, he ought also to have indicated that it was only a sample. The card which accompanied the wallets bore his secretary's Social Security account number. Later, his secretary was distinguished by becoming the only person in the history of the Social

Security program to have her number withdrawn and to be issued a new one. This, because people were indeed using the cards which had accompanied their wallets. And thousands of them had been sold. F.I.C.A. taxes poured into that account over the years. It was never completely unscrambled. A generation later, IRS was still receiving tax returns from all over the country with that magic number on them. And I'd a suspicion that even now, almost sixty years later, there were still a few coming in.

A broad category, therefore, was similarly in order for me now, for credit purposes. Then it hit me. Some companies have a single account for the traveling expenses of key executives and they obtain multiple credit cards bearing the same account number for issuance to the persons in that category. Such a number, backed by the credit of a reputable corporation, would be accepted by the credit company's computer without question. I could see that an amendment in the area of Donald Elpat's place of employment would soon be in order. All that I had to do was to discover the proper company and its number.

I thought about it for a few minutes and came up with a possible avenue of research. Since I still had plenty of time, I got up then, turned on the tv and looked at an all-news channel. I was loath to get too far behind on the world's doings. It's always good to know whether there's a flood or a tornado rushing to compound your problems.

I watched for over an hour. There was nothing about a fugitive named BelPatri—not that I'd expected to make the national news—and nothing at all about Angra.

Then I heard a car pull up in front of the office. I switched off the set at about the same time that the car door slammed, and I went to the window and looked out. Then I dropped the curtain and I reached.

Nothing.

I returned to the bed, stretched out and kept reaching.

Nothing. Nothing. Sooner or later, though. I just had to remain receptive. . .

Nothing. Nothing. . .

Flicker.

The terminal in the office had been activated. The person was taking a room. The desk clerk was inserting a credit card. . .

. . . Coiling into the unit, I moved in a direct line to the credit company's computer.

I sought out the company accounts listings and ransacked them for multiple input numbers with good high ceilings on the amounts chargable in a day's time. . .

. . . Then I got fussy and looked for one that was easy to commit to memory.

There.

Elpat had found his place of employment.

Just as I coiled out, a wavering image of Ann presented itself to my mind's eye. Just a blink— *flickerclick*—and she was gone and I was staring at the ceiling and wondering again at the contents of the subconscious.

I committed the number firmly to mind, then turned the tv on again and watched for awhile.

Moving off. Pine pinched my nostrils. An incontinent bird decorated my bike. The day grew warm, but at least I had the wind to cool me somewhat through it. Traffic was moderate. I saw no truck dancers. . .

Donald Elpat had had no trouble at the vehicle rental place. He had decided upon a motorcycle for a number of reasons—one very good one being that they are not equipped with any devices which would make them show up on traffic data computers; another being that cycling had not been one of my hobbies in Florida, nor had I even done much of it in my previous life. It seemed that I might reasonably expect to take the opposition by surprise by doing it now. At some point in the past I had at least learned how, and these new ones were particularly easy. Rechargable at any Angra station, the one I selected was powered by ultra-highspeed flywheels which also provided a gyro effect that helped to give it road stability. Donald Elpat signed for it, and we were moving off.

Since I had already zigged, I decided that it was time to zag, and after I had crossed the river I headed to the northwest, for Little Rock.

Yes, the memories had been there, of the occasions when I had biked in the past. They had started back in college, with Ann. We had occasionally continued them, afterwards:

Down in the pine barrens, eating our lunch under the trees. . .

"I'm beginning to feel funny about this work, Ann. But of course you know that."

"Yes. But what can I tell you that I did not tell you before?"

"You never told me before that Marie was going to be wrecking other people's research."

Her brows fluttered in puzzlement, like dark wings.

"But it is sometimes necessary, to maintain our lead."

"I thought that the whole point to all our pilferage was that once we had what we needed we could cut through all the rivalries and begin producing cheap energy faster than anybody else."

"That is correct."

"But if other people are gaining on us to the point where we have to set them back, it means that maybe they could do a better job than us if they were left alone. Maybe our whole premise is wrong."

"You thinking of changing employers?"

"No. I'm thinking that maybe we've got enough of an edge that we don't really have to step on the competition. After all—"

"A clear superiority," she interrupted, sounding like Barbeau now. "We have to be so far ahead that nobody can impede us in the slightest way. Only that will permit us to move quickly and efficiently to save the economy and maintain a high quality of life."

"You're talking monopoly, you know."

"If that's what it takes, what of it? The alternative is chaos."

"Maybe so," I said. "Maybe you're right. I don't know any more. I guess I never knew for certain. And what about this Matthews, anyway? What does he do? There's something vaguely sinister about him."

"He is a highly specialized technician," she said, "and his work is even more secret than ours."

"But you can read his mind. Is he trustworthy?"

"Oh yes," she said. "He can always be relied upon

to do what he says. I'd trust him with my life."

I was again persuaded for a time. Some birds were singing. Angra continued to tick along, like a bomb within my mind. I learned a little about bikes in those days, anyway.

I rested in Little Rock that afternoon and chowed down on junk food. Then, batteries recharged, having zagged, it was time to zig again, headed for Dallas, ears buzzing, body vibrating.

Moving off, the beat of the road filling me, my mind went back again, to those last days at Angra. I had learned of Willy Boy's talent, but still I stayed on, actually buying Barbeau's explanation that Matthews only incapacitated the competition, putting out researchers with unexplained fainting spells, resurgences of ulcers, false angina pains, temporary blindness, aphasia, bouts of the flu, transient neuropathies of various sorts. Then, one day, on its way from Double Z to destruction, I had come upon the kill order for an executive in a rival company. The only reason it even caught my attention was that I had read the man's obituary that morning and the name stood out. He had died of heart failure. I'd even met him once. He was young and had seemed healthy. The order had only gone to Willy Boy the day before. There was no way this could be a coincidence. . .

I stormed into Barbeau's office. At first he denied it. Then he admitted it and tried to explain that the action was necessary, the man too dangerous.

"Too dangerous to go on living?" I shouted.

"Now listen, Steve. Calm down. You've got to understand the big picture. . ."

He moved around his desk and tried to put his hand on my shoulder, assuming one of his paternalistic poses. I knocked it away.

"I *am* starting to understand the big picture. That's what's bothering me. I've done a lot for good old Angra—a lot of things I felt badly about—but I always consoled myself that a lot of good was going to come out of it all. Now I find out you're killing people, too! Damn it! We're not at war! We've got to draw the line somewhere—"

The door opened then and two company guards entered. Barbeau had obviously signaled for them when I'd started getting loud. Unfortunately for them I was in the mood to hit something. Right after I'd gotten out of the hospital, after the accident, I'd started in martial arts classes, to build up my muscle tone, my coordination. I'd never stopped, because I'd taken a liking to it. I'd switched disciplines a number of times over the years. I had a whole battery of reflexes.

I left both guards unconscious and Barbeau trying to tell me that Matthews was always quick and merciful. I stalked out and went back to see Big Mac. Before I was taken at gunpoint, I had transmitted the entire contents of our Double Z file to the Interstate Commerce Commission's computer.

I was held prisoner for three days after that, and I was not physically abused. First, he sent Ann to try to talk me back into the fold, but I was onto her trick of seeing my objections before I voiced them and having the best possible reply ready. This time it was a little different. She couldn't change the facts and I wasn't buying anything she had on the menu. She seemed saddened by my attitude, as if I were blaming her personally for everything.

Willy Boy himself actually came around later, and I thought that the show was over for me. But not yet. In an almost eloquent way, interspersed with Biblical quotations which didn't really apply, he tried to justify himself. Angra was the Chosen People and he was the Joshua for Barbeau's Moses. For a moment, he almost seemed pathetic, but then I remembered how much he got paid for his expertise.

"You're talking in tongues about nothing of interest to me," I told him. "And you don't really believe all that yourself."

He smiled.

"Okay, Steve. How 'bout lookin' at it this way, then—Marie and me, we just mess up the competition. You and Ann are the ones who really bring in the goodies. The stuff you bring home is more technical and more important. That makes you important. Forget about what you might think are right and wrong. You're on the winning side. You can write your own ticket, not skitter around like a hog on ice. If you still feel bad ten years from now, when you're really on top, that'll be the time to repent. You'll be in a position for all kinds of good works to ease your conscience. I know all about consciences. . ."

I shook my head.

"I just don't see it that way."

He sighed. He shrugged.

"All righty. I can tell The Boss I tried. Want a drink?"

"Yeah."

He passed me his hip flask and I took a pull. He took a generous one himself before he restored it to his pocket.

"Go ahead," I said. "Get it over with."

He looked startled.

"Sorry if I made that seem like your last meal. I've got no orders to send you to your reward yet."

"Do you know what Barbeau's going to do with me?"

"Nope. He hasn't said. See you around."

And that was the last time I'd seen him till he tried to kill me in Philadelphia.

It wasn't until later that Barbeau, flanked by armed guards, gave me the pitch himself, in very obvious sociological terms. My answer was still the same.

He pursed his lips.

"What are we going to do with you, Steve?"

"I can guess."

"I'd rather not. Hate to see a talent like yours wasted, especially when you could change your mind one day. Who knows what time might bring?"

"You going to keep me locked up for a few years to find out?"

"I was thinking of a more congenial way for you to pass the time."

"Oh?"

"How would you like to be someone else?"

"What do you mean?"

"I can't have you walking around, knowing everything you know. My contacts at ICC were able to dispose of your message properly. At least, I think that matter's closed. Hate to have to send Willy Boy to Washington at this point. He should never have to waste his time there on anything less than a congressman." He chuckled at his own wit. "Now, I can't just wait around and wonder what you'll do next time. So you've just earned yourself a very long leave of absence—maybe permanent.''

"Meaning?"

"A good doctor can do wonders with hypnosis and drugs. New identity. A whole new set of memories. It's even easier, I understand, if the patient is cooperative. Now, if the alternative is death and the new life promises to be one long, pleasant vacation, what would any sane man say?''

"You've got a point there," I said, after a time.

. . . And I dreamed of Baghdad and awoke to palm trees.

I watched the sun go down, lighting low clouds. I was tired. My crazy sleep schedule of the past few days was getting to me. The lights of advancing traffic became a molten stream in my aching eyes. There was no sense in pushing on to Dallas and arriving dead beat. I located a motel outside Texarkana, came up with another new name and paid cash again, just to be cautious. I showered, went out and found a diner, ate, came back and went to bed.

That should have been the end of it for the day, but as I lay there, drifting between sleep and wakefulness, my mind moved toward the nearest focus of data processing activity. A telex, receiving reservations, was chattering away somewhere nearby.

Chatter-tet-ter.

. . . *Low-level stuff, hardly even recreational for the semi-conscious. Yet I drifted with it—somewhere. . .*

"Hello"—*flat and mechanical, her entire being. For a moment, I forgot that she was dead. . .*

"Hi, Ann."

"Hello."

. . . Slowly, an awareness that something was wrong came over me. Her image was superimposed upon a twinkling array of lights—a magic loom? consciousness weaving?

Memory crept back.

"What happened?" I asked her.

"Happened . . ." she repeated. "I am—here."

"How do you feel?"

"Feel . . . Where are my flowers?"

"Oh, they're around. What—what have you been doing?"

"I am not all here," she said then, as if just discovering it. "I—doing? Waking. I think—waking. Waking up."

"Is there something you want?"

"Yes."

"What?"

"I do not know. More. Yes, more. And my flowers. . ."

"Where are you?"

"I am—here. I—"

. . . And then the lights faded and she was gone.

I woke up and thought about it for a time. It had seemed as if she were somehow being turned into a computer program. Not a terribly advanced one, at this point. It seemed as if her mind were somehow preserved in a manner similar to a body's being maintained on a heart-lung machine. Basic, low-level functioning. How? Why?

I was too tired to return to the data-net and look for answers. A deep, black sleep was rushing toward me. . .

I cast my plans over an early breakfast. Whether it was impatience or a hunch, I decided to switch modes of transportation in Dallas if I could. I was beginning to feel more confidence in my abilities.

From breakfast to Dallas was not a bad ride; a bit dusty in places, a bit gusty in others, but I made it out to the big Dallas-Ft. Worth Airport in good time. I left the bike in the lot there and found out from an information unit the section of the terminal from which the Dallas to El Paso shuttle departed. I also learned that it routinely stopped at Carlsbad and at Angra Test Facility Number Four. Then I cleaned myself up, had lunch at a counter and rode the monorail to the proper building.

When I arrived, I studied the posted schedule. There were several shuttle flights that afternoon and evening.

Then I went and sat down in a deserted section of the waiting area. I could feel all of the computer activity around me. Since Angra was responsible for this whole damned trip, I decided that they ought to start footing the bill.

I coiled and worked my way eastward through the data-net. Nothing as spectacular as my earlier raid on Big Mac was in order now. The information I wanted would not be in Double Z. By comparison, it would almost be lying about in plain sight. I was still very fresh on the first, outer layer of defenses, and I passed through them like smoke through a window screen.

Angra, too, had multiple-input credit accounts— different ones for different executive levels. I selected a sufficiently high one that it might give me priority on the shuttle—like bumping some lower-grade executive—as Angra appeared to be a steady customer with reserved blocs of seats on the thing. Then, in a whimsical mood, I added Donald Elpat to the list of Angra executives entitled to use that account. Even if the airline were to check back now, I had my bona fides. But why go halfway?

Next, I instructed Big Mac to make the reservation for Elpat, for a seat on the next shuttle. I waited for a confirmation.

I coiled out then, jotted the account number on a scrap of paper from my wallet and rehearsed it until I could call it quickly to mind. Then I went over to the desk, told the man I was Elpat and that I wanted my ticket. I passed him my doctored card at which he did not even glance, save to orient it and insert it into a slot before him. I controlled the signal, and a moment later my ticket emerged from an adjacent slot. He handed it to me.

"It's not going to be landing at Angra today, though," he said.

"Oh?"

"They've closed the place. The nearest you can get off is at Carlsbad."

"How come?"

He shrugged.

"Some sort of testing, I believe."

"Okay. Thanks."

"That gate over there," he said, gesturing. "In about forty minutes."

While I waited, I decided to have a cup of coffee from a machine across the way. When I got there and began fishing around, however, I discovered that I did not have the proper change. Suddenly, the machine clicked and hummed. A cup descended onto the gridwork and began to fill. Black, the way I liked it.

I smelled violets, and then heard Ann's voice, as if she were standing beside me.

"Fortify yourself," she said. "I'm buying."

The violets had faded and the sense of her presence had vanished before the cup was completely filled. I didn't know what to make of that one. But, "Thanks," I said, as I raised the plastic hatch and took the steaming cup back to the waiting area. It couldn't be larceny, I decided later, since it's a bigger crime to take anyone's money for that bad a cup of coffee.

I studied the other people who were gradually populating the waiting area. The possibility had only just occurred to me that someone I had known back in my Angra days might be on the flight. Barbeau had kept his little group of specialists pretty much apart from the regular run of employees; but still, we were all acquainted with some of them. Most of my associates, though, had been in data processing and none of them seemed to be about. It was not difficult to tell who the Angra people were, though. One had but to listen for a few moments. They were the ones bitching about having to get off in Carlsbad and wait around, eating and drinking and loafing at company expense, poor devils.

We finally boarded, and I sequestered myself behind a magazine. The automatic takeoff was uneventful, as was the first half hour or so of the flight. Then, suddenly, Ann was talking to me and I closed my eyes and saw her, standing beneath a highly polished-looking tree with a mirrorlike finish, clusters of metal flowers about her, gleaming with machine oil, riveted to the surface on which she stood. And she stood there as if at attention, eyes straight ahead, arms down at her sides, heels together.

"It's, it's, it's," she said. "It knows you."

"What does?" I said mentally.

"It which is. It gardened me here. It would care."

"But what is it?"

"It's . . . It knows you."

"But I don't know it."

"Yes you do."

"Tell me about it."

". . . Going again," I heard her say. "Back again, stronger. . ."

And then she was gone.

Carlsbad finally came into view. I had the impression of an oasis on a small brown river, set in the midst of a hot, lunar-looking landscape. As we flew nearer, I noted a lot of new construction around the edges of the town, a good indication that it was growing fast.

Then we began to descend for a landing at a little field perhaps twenty kilometers out of town. Again, some of my fellow passengers began to complain. I could have taken over the autopilot and forced the shuttle to land us at Angra's own field. I'd a feeling they would be a lot more disturbed at what happened to them if I were to do that.

It gave me an idea, though, that train of thought. It was no difficult trick to slip into the flight computer as we were landing and to activate a temporarily proscribed program which was already there.

The shuttle took off quickly after we had disembarked, once the field about it was cleared. It was on its way to Angra's own field. I wondered whether they really believed I was stupid enough to approach them in that manner. It should prove mildly diverting, at any rate. I wondered how afraid of me they might have become. I kept my mind open for impressions, following the progress of the empty vehicle.

Later, as the bus bore us into town, I felt the sudden destruction of the shuttle during its descent pattern. I couldn't tell what they'd hit it with—lasers, solar mirrors—but it went fast.

Nervous, I'd say.

Good.

I decided not to keep them in suspense too much longer. The Yellow Pages and a street guide told me everything I needed. I walked to a shop where they rented me a simple bicycle, and then I headed out of town to the southeast. Moving off.

FIFTEEN

The afternoon burned about me. I should have bought a hat, I realized, to protect my head from that sunglare. And the pedalling got to be hard work before very long.

I followed the signs, and when I got to within a few kilometers of the facility I passed off to the side into the first patch of shade I came to, beside a high yellow and orange section of embankment at the bottom of a dip in the road. I waited there until I stopped perspiring and my breathing returned to normal. Then I waited a little longer.

It was unfortunate that I had never visited this particular installation during my time at Angra. I had no idea as to its layout. I only knew that it covered a pretty large area. I began wondering how many people were in there now. Not too many, I guessed. When you've got a baited deathtrap ready, you like to keep the number of its operators to a minimum. It was awkward to accumulate wit-nesses. On the other hand, this made it likely that everyone on the premises was very dangerous. Shee-it, as Willy Boy was wont to observe.

I walked the bike up the slope and mounted again when I reached the top.

In the distance, I saw the place, and a high metal fence separated it from the rest of the world, like a border around a private country. There was a small security shed outside the gate toward which I was headed, but I could detect no signs of activity in or about it. There seemed to be nothing behind the fence that resembled a weapon aimed in my direction either. In fact, there was no activity at all behind the fence. The place looked deserted.

I reached out as I rode toward it. I seemed to detect a little computer activity far off, but it was too distant to mean anything to me.

There was scant cover beside the road, but I marked it all as I passed. A useless exercise, as it turned out. Nothing threatened my approach. I kept right on until I came up beside the shed, where I leaned the bicycle. I looked inside. No one home.

The gate even stood obligingly ajar, opened just enough for a man on foot to slide through the space without touching anything.

A couple of dozen meters inside, an unpretentious administration building stood, one-story, fairly new-looking, the face of efficiency. It was fronted by a small lawn, a few trees and bushes. There was also a pair of fountains, flanking the walk—demonstrating a small but conspicuous waste of energy. I heard Angra's message to the world in their soft plattering: Energy is not going to be a problem ever again. Plenty of the stuff here. If you're buying, we're selling.

I didn't trust that gate. It was just too damned obvious a situation. I coiled forward, feeling for anything trap-like in the vicinity.

I traced the electric sensors that held a killing voltage ready to apply across the gap whenever a human body might pass through—and the relay that at the same time would swing the gate a few inches shut, making deadly contact.

So much for the obvious. Traps within traps, wheels within wheels . . . All right. Some other way then.

Back in the security shed I had seen some one-person flyers—awkward, difficult little things with rotors like helicopters, and flywheels like the new motorcycles for power and some semblance of stability. I went back and regarded them. I probed, but I could detect no booby-traps. I'd be damned if I'd try flying one in, though. One of Barbeau's hobbies had been skeet shooting.

I jiggled the controls until I got one of them out of the shed on its own power. Then I left it hovering in mid-air and went back for another. After that, I decided on one more. Three seemed the maximum that I could manipulate, like juggling balls.

I moved a bit nearer to the gate and readied myself.

Then I sent one spinning aloft, high over the fence, crashed another into the fence right near the gate and summoned the third to my side, moving as if to mount it.

The results were spectacular.

The fence made a noise like frying bacon and the one flyer looked amazingly like an exotic insect imbedded in a burning web. Meanwhile, there was a flash as of heat lightning from somewhere beyond

the building and I heard the other flyer crash out o
sight.

Then, accompanied by metallic odors, I jammed
the electric relays and rushed toward the gate on
foot. Only as I was passing through it, did I realize
that there was a simpler, well-protected trigger that
I had missed—but it had been shorted out by the
flyer I had crashed into the fence. My luck, or something, was still functioning.

I raced toward the bushes that fringed the building, as if seeking to approach it from the side or the
rear—and I kept right on going. It seemed a very
likely place for Willy Boy to be waiting, and I
wanted to keep a lot more distance than the width of
a revival tent between us.

As I rounded the building, I saw a drainage ditch a
dozen paces to my left. I ran and dove into it. No
shots rang over my head. The only sound was that of
a dry, wandering wind. I reached. . .

Computer activity, ahead, far to the right. . .

I coiled, fast.

I found my way into the data underpinnings for
what had to be a projected map of the complex. I
quickly back-translated it into mental imagery. I
saw the command post—a very mechanized
place—housing the computer and probably Barbeau himself, farther to the south. The presence of a
helicopter, engine turning over, was indicated on
the ground beside it. Was he getting ready to go aloft
to try spotting me from the air? Or was it a ready
means of escape if things began breaking in my favor
and it suddenly became too hot for him on the premises?

Along the way in which I was headed, I saw that

there were two strategically situated buildings where ambushes had been set. I might avoid one but not both. I ignored them for the moment, for I saw that the position where I had gone to earth, my present position, was also clearly indicated. I had to do something about that fast. I traced the signal that activated the notation. It took me a while to realize where it was coming from, but when I did I raised my head a bit and viewed the thing.

In the distance, some sort of unit was rotating atop a high tower. I got the impression that it might be doing a sonar scan of the area, tracking and registering anything above a certain size that moved.

Okay. I had to find a way to juggle the local power supply, hit it with a surge and burn it out. This was trickier than I'd thought it would be, and it took me the better part of two minutes.

I crawled on quickly then, postponing further scrutiny of the terrain via the computer until I'd altered my position somewhat. Another quick glance showed me that the thing on the tower had stopped rotating, and I was pleased to see that my position-marker had vanished from the map-analogue. I crawled along the ditch for over a hundred meters, passing a building which had not been shown as occupied when I had regarded the layout.

Behind that building lay the airstrip. There were four hangars and a number of pads with 'copters upon them. On the airstrip lay the remains of the shuttle I had sent on from Carlsbad, partly melted. They had waited until it was almost on the ground before they'd wasted it. They hadn't wanted a public disaster out on public land to draw attention and reporters and emergency vehicles and crews. They wanted to keep the party private. That was all right with me, too. I found myself getting even angrier than I had been.

No matter which direction I took from here, I would have to pass one of the ambush points in order to penetrate farther into the complex. I coiled again.

Yes. The nearest was just beyond the next building opposite the field. The computer showed three persons waiting there, as at the other ambush point.

I crawled a little farther, until I had interposed the nearest building directly between myself and the next one, effectively blocking any line of sight.

Then I rose and ran, flattening myself against the side of the building when I reached it. I waited for several heartbeats, but nothing happened. I moved to the nearest window then and tried to raise it. Locked.

I tapped it with a stone until it shattered, reached inside and unlatched it. I raised it, hoping that distance and the wind had smothered the sound.

I climbed inside and closed it again, then moved on through toward the other side. It was some sort of electrical shop, I saw immediately from the tools and components spread along the benches which lined the walls. There was nothing among it all which might serve as a real weapon, though, so I passed quickly—past storage racks and bins to a small office area.

I peered around the edge of the window at the building across the way. Both of its windows on the side facing me were open, and there were people inside holding what I had to assume were weapons.

All right. The gloves were off, the brass knuckles were on.

Dropping to the floor, I crawled to the window on the wall to my left and checked it out, also. Still nothing there but the open, barren expanse which had lain before me on the way over. I flipped the latch and raised that window, slowly.

Then I sat down, my back against the wall, and I reached. . .

Brekekekex. . .

. . . The helicopter stirred on its pad, rose, headed this way, picking up speed. It swung into a wide curve, out over the administration building, the fence, coming back this way now, picking up speed, descending . . . I heard it clearly now. . .

It swooped down like a dark angel and crashed full into the facing side of the adjacent building.

I was over the sill in an instant and I hit the ground running. The earth was still vibrating from the impact, and pieces still fell about the stove-in wall. The tail assembly of the 'copter protruded, still twisting, from the dust-filled cavern it had created. I saw no signs of the ambushers as I raced on past.

I pumped my arms and kept going. Soon the ruined building was far behind me and the other ambush point was even farther away —to the right, to my rear. I kept on. The facility stretched away for miles before me. The prospect began to widen, also, installations occurring now to my left in addition to the simpler buildings to my right, with more exotic structures towering far ahead. I felt more and more computerized activity about me as I advanced.

Finally, I had to halt to catch my breath. I swerved toward a four-story Maypole of a power plant model, a silvery mesh of webwork hung about it like a shawl. I crouched in a recessed area behind a burnished housing, beneath a flight of steel stairs. I was afforded a distant view of a turning geodesic dome, each of its faces a different color.

"Stephenson McFarland!" Barbeau's voice boomed, and echoes of the words came from all over the installation.

I saw that there was a bitch-box bolted to an upright along the stair just above my head, a part of a general public address system covering the entire complex, it seemed.

"Stephenson McFarland!"

. . . I'd recognized it at once as my proper name. And hearing it seemed to cause all of the remaining pieces of my memory to fall into their proper places. . .

"I'd like to call this whole thing off right now," Barbeau stated. "I made a mistake, Steve—back at the Philly airport. I'm sorry for that and I want to apologize. I don't want to kill you now. Listen to me. You can see that I wouldn't want such a thing any more. I had no idea how much you'd—changed."

Ha! Good to have him sweating it now. He'd never have chosen a place like this for our confrontation had he realized what I could do with the machines. And I had just taken away his helicopter so that he couldn't flee easily. I'd bet he'd like to have me back on his side.

". . . Surely you can see that I want you alive now," he continued. "It would be impossible for me to want you otherwise, under the present circumstances. Especially now that Ann's been lost to us. You've got a really good future waiting for you with Angra. . ."

I coiled into his computer again—a rush of colored lights—and I refrained from using the CRT display on which he was seeking me on grid after grid— apparently as yet unaware that I had knocked out his sonar eye—for purposes of transmitting an over-printed obscenity I had strongly in mind. Instead, I sought after any building that was heavily moni-tored. There was such a place, and I plunged into its systems.

CORA. She had entered her name into the local unit through which she must communicate with her captors. Of course, it was enough. She must know something about my abilities now, doubtless a re-sult of many questions she had been asked. I won-dered what her mind now held concerning me. It came to me as a real shock then, how much I must have changed during the past few days. For me it was simply remembering, but—I realized that I was no longer the man she had known down in the Keys. He had been something of a vegetable so far as I was now concerned, but a fraction of myself. I was smarter and tougher and—probably somewhat nas-tier. Would she still care about me if she knew what I was really like? It mattered, quite a bit, for I realized that, if anything, I cared even more for her now.

Tentatively, with something like fear, I took over control of the home unit with the tv screen which seemed there to entertain her and through which she was watched. The overprint trick I had almost used to swear at Barbeau served me then.

CORA. ARE YOU ALL RIGHT? DON, I caused it to display.

It was almost a minute before she noticed it, during which time I was subjected to more of Barbeau's pleas that I listen to reason, that I rejoin the team. . .

When she spotted my message she activated the keyboard through which she controlled the environment of her prison, requested special programming, communicated with her captors. . .

YES, she typed. WHERE ARE YOU?

SOMEWHERE NEAR, I THINK. WHERE ARE YOU?

She typed:

TEST RANGE. SOLAR-POWER LASER PERIMETER DEFENSE. LOTS OF SLAG HEAPS.

HANG IN THERE, I answered. I MAY BE A WHILE. AUFWIEDERSEHEN.

I checked through the main computer's catalog of ongoing projects, learning what some of those bizarre structures in the distance were.

". . . At a substantial pay increase," Barbeau was saying.

"Where's Cora? I want to talk to Cora!" I called out, for I had checked and I knew that the PA system worked both ways.

I knew that I was giving away my position for the moment, but at this point it didn't matter to me. I wanted his reaction.

"Steve!" came the reply. "She's here. She's all right. In fact, she's really frightened at what you might be going to do."

"Let me talk to her then." I had to ask that. I didn't want him guessing that I'd already been in touch with her.

"In time, in good time," he said. "But first—"

"I'll wait," I said, and I took off running.

I had been able to check while he was talking, and I knew now where the solar-powered laser perimeter defense test area was located. I also had a picture of what the thing was: It was a military research project, where laser power packs were charged by the sun. Apparently, the accumulated energy could be released like a lightning bolt. Details. Deal with that later. . .

I ran toward that no man's land with the strange structures. She was back there in a furnished observer's hut in the test range area. Dirt roads with names like St. James Place, Park Place, Baltic Avenue and Boardwalk twisted through the lunar landscape over gray and white, limestone and fossil soil, where the tough, enduring vegetation looked three-quarters dead in the dry heat. There was wealth here—oil under the earth, and potash—and there was stored nuclear waste buried in ancient salt beds not far away, I remembered. I recalled the irony in what seemed the company's namesake, which I had once looked up—Angra Mainyu, in Persian mythology, was in the final analysis an anti-sun deity, a corrupter of that which he touched, the destroyer of the tree of life. When I pointed this out to Barbeau, he just laughed and said no, it stood for Allied Naturally Generated Radiation Assets and one shouldn't waste time looking for paradoxes and subtleties where simple answers suffice.

The sun beat down fiercely as I passed among experimental solar-electrical pilot plants of various kinds. There were vats and towers and pyramids and banks of slanted sheets. There were structures with slowly turning paddles, emulating leaves I supposed. Some of them I'd never even heard of. And

out farther—"near the slag heaps"—was Cora's
prison.

". . . We're going to have to come to terms,
Steve," Barbeau's voice said, from a dusky Christ-
mas tree of a structure off to my left. "We need each
other. . ."

I turned at the corner of Mediterranean and
Ventnor Avenues. I met her under a solar mirror.
She was wearing a long black robe with a golden
dragon on the breast.

"Ann!"

"I have found strength," she said, a little less flatly
than on recent occasions. "They are coming for you
now—the three men from the other house. One of
them, their point man, is very near." She turned her
head and I followed her gaze toward a low building
bristling with antennae over on Marvin Gardens.
"Do you know what 'kinetic-triggering'
means. . . ?"

I saw nothing in that direction and when I turned
back again Ann was gone.

I took off toward that crouched porcupine of a
structure, all of my senses alert. I thought that I
knew what she meant. I'd read about research on a
computerized laser hand weapon. It could be set to
fire automatically at fast-moving objects. It was
said that it could even be set to shoot down in flight
an ordinary bullet aimed at its holder. The thing
could also be used in conjunction with a helmet-
headband, adjusted to fire at the point where its
operator fixed his gaze. All of which meant that I
was a dead man as soon as a line of sight opened
between us. . .

So . . . I coiled, seeking that electronic viper-
brain somewhere ahead.

Tzzz. . .

. . . It was moving slowly, stage right, along the far side of the porcupine. But no computer, no laser beam performing its deadly dance. I turned it off and held it that way. I kept running.

When the man stepped into view, I saw that he was holding what looked like an oversized harmonica in a vertical position in his right hand. He wore a metal headband about his dark locks, and there was some sort of lead running from it to a power pack on his belt, another from that unit to the thing in his hand.

After several moments his face fell and he began to shake the weapon. He slapped at the power pack.

He tried to use the thing as a club when I closed with him. I parried the blow and caught him on the temple with one knuckle, hard. He fell.

I stripped off his weapon gear and donned it myself. I reactivated the little computer as I took hold of the grip at the rear of the harmonica. Then I moved to the side of the porcupine and was about to seek the other two units.

The thing vibrated almost imperceptibly in my hand and I heard a cry.

To my left and perhaps thirty meters across the way, beside a big black metal housing surrounded by giant ceramic pots, two people lay sprawled. They both wore headbands and neither was moving. I coiled and turned off their weapons. Then I advanced upon them, my own deadly harmonica at ready.

They were dead, though. I was appalled at the quiet efficiency of the thing that I held. I hadn't even seen my would-be attackers. If I had, I would have wrecked their weapons. Then I could probably have broken them a leg apiece and at least left them alive. I wanted to throw the thing away, but I was afraid that I might still need it.

I turned back to the dessicated plain, facing in the direction of the testing range.

". . . There's no reason for all of this," Barbeau's voice boomed after me. "We solved the energy problem, didn't we, Steve? When you worked for Angra, you did a great service for your country, for all of Western civilization. There are still great things ahead. We can still deal."

"Let Cora go now," I called out, "and you'll still be alive when we leave here! That's my deal!"

"Steve! Wait! I can promise you a completely different setup than last time! You'll like this one!"

"Cora! Now!" I shouted into the next speaker I passed.

"I can't, Steve!"

"Why not?"

"She's my only insurance against you!"

"Damn it! I said I'd leave you alone if you give her to me!"

"That's a frail thing to lean on, boy!"

"My word? I wouldn't have left Angra if I didn't have a few principles. My word is good!"

"Now let's calm down a bit! I still want a deal, too. . ."

I ignored him and kept going. I passed something that looked like a house of cards, another structure that was all piping with liquids gurgling inside. . .

The weapon moved in my hand, and something burned in the air to my right. I was left with the outline of a monkey wrench within the afterimage.

That, and a puddle of something molten on the ground. Where had it come from? Who could have thrown. . .

Suddenly, the harmonica was stirring again, and a myriad of bright points filled the air—screwdrivers, pliers, crowbars, hammers . . . It was as if someone had fired the entire contents of a tool chest in my direction. The damned little thing burned them all.

There was a shed far off to my right, near a funny-smelling chemical-electrical installation.

"Marie!" I called, the picture suddenly coming clear. "Don't come out! This thing will burn anything that moves!"

"I get the idea!" I heard her shout. "How's about pointing it the other way?"

"Why should I?"

" 'Cause you win!" she called back. "I just quit my job with Angra about half a minute ago! Let me walk out of this place and I won't bother you any more!"

"I wish I could believe you!"

"I wish you would, too! I was dirt poor, Steve! I bet you never were! I didn't like what I had to do to make all that money, but I did it anyway! Because poor was even worse! I never much liked the rest of you, because it didn't seem to bother you! Not the way it bothered me! This seems like a good time to quit! Let me go!"

"You waited a long time!" I said.

"Not too long, I hope! Can I come out?"

I switched off the weapon's computer.

"Okay! Come ahead!"

She stepped out of the shed. She was wearing

jeans and a red blouse. Her face was a dark, tense mask. She turned to her left and began walking back toward the front of the compound.

"I left my bicycle by the security shed outside," I said. "You can take it."

"Thanks."

"And Barbeau heard every word we said. Don't get too near that building he's in. He's nasty enough to take a shot at you."

She nodded.

"I think I'm going to open a restaurant," she said. "You come by one day.

"And watch out for the preacher," she added. "He's still around—somewhere."

I adjusted the weapon to its simpler mode and covered her till she was out of sight. But nothing threatened.

I moved on, searching the area again for abnormal computer activity. Nothing special registered. Just the *kapocketing* of the various test plants. I reversed my earlier strategy now, staying out in the open, away from nooks and crannies where a fat man with death in his mind could be hiding. I tuned out Barbeau's monologue for a time. I passed the last of the big installations and before me lay a wasteland, just a few smaller bits of equipment here and there, and a few scattered huts. In the farther distance there were slag heaps.

There were also a few towers with speakers attached. . .

Well, one more time:

"Listen," I said. "I just killed three of your men with those fancy guns and Marie is no longer with you. I took out the other three, too, in case you hadn't noticed. You don't have that much left. I know where Cora is. Call off Matthews. Patch in Cora's hut and let's make this a conference call. I want to make plans for getting out of here with a minimum of fuss. You go your way and we'll go ours. What do you say?"

"If you mean that, give me back the computer," he answered.

"What do you mean?"

"It's just gone crazy."

"Must be a malfunction," I said. "I'm not doing it."

"I don't believe you."

"Wait a minute."

I spun through the Coil Effect. He was right. There was a massive computer malfunction in progress. Readings were skewed, systems were breaking down. . .

"I see it but I'm not doing it," I said. "Let me check further."

I dropped quickly from level to level, coming finally to the most basic place.

"It's being caused by power surges," I said. "Your generator's acting up."

"What should I do?"

"Go back to New Jersey. We'll send you a postcard from the Caribbean."

"Stop it, Steve!"

"Screw you, Barbeau," I said.

I coiled again, into the systems in the shed ahead. It was a great place to keep a prisoner. Sufficiently isolated that hundreds of employees could go about their business during normal work days without suspecting anything, it had its own plumbing and food supply and airconditioning and limited communications unit. It seemed as if it had actually been designed for occasional use as a cell. Knowing Angra as I now did, I was sure that this was not the first time it had functioned in this capacity.

I froze when I read the latest message Cora had entered into the home unit:

A FAT MAN IS HIDING BEHIND THE SLAG HEAP AT THE WEST SIDE OF THE HOUSE.

That was it then. The killing power of the thing I carried had a greater range than Matthews did. And he was not a fool. I ought to be able to back him down.

"Steve! Steve!" Barbeau began to scream. "The place is on fire!"

"Then get your ass out of there!"

"I can't! You've jammed the door!"

"I didn't jam anything!"

I coiled again, but the computer was still crazy and was rapidly degenerating even further. I did manage to discover that it was a fancy electronic lock on the control center door, though, and it was indeed jammed.

"There is nothing that I can do!" I said. "You're too far away! Get hold of a fire extinguisher and try to break out!"

"Stop it, Steve! I'll let her go! I'll do it your way!"

"I didn't start it! I can't stop it! Smash a window! Jump! Anything!"

"They're grilled over!"

"I'm sorry!" I said. "I'm helpless!"

"I'll get you yet!" he cried, just a few seconds before the power failed entirely.

But that few seconds was enough.

A flash like a sudden bolt of lightning blinded me. The hut toward which I was headed collapsed and began to smoulder. I heard a man scream. The public address system went dead. I began to run.

The flames were only just beginning as I pushed my way through the wreckage, but I knew that the place would soon be a mass of fire. I pulled at a section of wall. I moved a fallen beam. I saw her there, lying there, still.

I heaved at the rubble which still covered her. I could not tell whether she was breathing. There were smoke and flames all about me by the time I had her free. I picked her up and made my way back out of the ruin. Now I knew what a laser perimeter defense did.

I heard moaning as I left what remained of the building. Matthews was lying on the ground about forty feet away. I lowered Cora and felt for her pulse. It was weak. She was breathing shallowly. Her right arm looked broken. Her scalp and forehead were badly lacerated. I raised her eyelids, having read a lot of neurological literature during my incapacitation. Her right pupil was a pinpoint; her left one was normal-sized. I began wiping blood from her face and arm.

"Cora!" I said. "Can you hear me?"

There was no reply. I rubbed her wrists. I tried to place her into the most comfortable position. . .

"Steve!"

I turned my head. Willy Boy, badly burned, was propped on an elbow. The left side of his face looked charred. His left eye was closed. His garments still smoked.

"Come here," he croaked.

"You've got to be kidding. I don't need a coronary, thanks."

"I won't hurt you . . . Please."

I looked at Cora. I looked back at him. I couldn't think of anything else to do for her.

There was something peculiar about Matthews—and then I realized what it was.

I stood.

"Okay," I said. "But you listen to me first. I can feel that little gadget in your chest working overtime. Maybe you know now what I can do to machines. I'll come and see what I can do for you. But if I feel the least pain in my chest I'm going to turn your pacemaker off." I snapped my fingers. "Like that."

He grinned weakly as I left Cora and moved toward him.

"You might call this a heart to heart talk then," he said.

As I moved nearer, he began reciting numbers and then he said something in German.

"Get that?" he finished.

"No."

"If you've got something to write with, write 'em down. Please."

"What are they?"

He said them again and I scribbled them onto the same piece of paper from my wallet that I'd used for my phoney Angra account number.

". . . And Maggie Sims in Atlanta," he said hoarsely. "Here's her phone number. . ."

"What is all this?"

"She's my sister—the only family I got left. Call her and give her the name of my Swiss bank and that number. I hate to see all that money go to waste. . ."

"Shit!" I said. "Your dirty money can rot in Switzerland and your sister in Atlanta! You killed Ann and you tried to kill me! The hell with you!"

I turned away and headed back for Cora. Then I halted.

"Willy Boy . . ." I said. "Maybe we can make a deal."

"What?" he whispered.

"You used to be in the healing business. Do it for Cora and I'll call your sister. I'll tell her what you said."

"Steve, I ain't done that in years."

"Do it now."

He was silent for a little while. Then, "Bring her over," he said, "and I'll give it a try."

I went back to Cora. She was still breathing, shallowly. I gathered her up and carried her over to Willy Boy. I set her down beside him.

"Okay," I said.

"Prop me up against this pile of stuff, will you?"

He was heavy, but I managed to shift him into a sitting position against the nearest mound of slag. He bit his lip and remained silent while I did it. But then he began coughing. It went on for awhile.

Then, "Can you turn me a bit to the left?" he said. "And then get my flask out of my hip pocket?"

I managed to roll him to the side. I located his flask. I pulled it from his pocket and unstoppered it. I began raising it to his lips, but he took it into his hand and guided it himself. He took a long pull, then began coughing again. When he stopped, he took another drink and then lowered it. He breathed heavily then for a moment and nodded.

"Okay," he said.

He looked at Cora, and then he grinned. He rolled his eyes upward in an expression of mock-piety.

"Got a minute, God?" he asked. "This here's old Willy Boy, prayin' off his regular network. Now our sister here is ailin'. . ."

"Cut it out," I said, feeling uncomfortable. "Just do it, huh?"

But he ignored me.

". . . An innocent child, so far as I know," he went on, "she just got herself in the wrong place at the wrong time. It's sad. I don't know if she's got faith and all that, or if it matters much any more. But how about a little grace and mercy and healin'?" He was still grinning. "Let's have a touch of the Spirit to ease her troubles . . ." He raised the flask and took another drink. "Now, we used to do this thing reg'lar together. Maybe for old times' sake and love and compassion and all that stuff—"

Suddenly his voice broke and he closed his good eye.

"Damn!" he said. "I feel the Spirit! I do feel it!"

His display bothered me more and more. I had never considered myself especially religious, but there seemed no reason for all this mockery and . . . whatever it was.

". . . So I'm gonna lay hands on our sister here," he said, and now his voice was changed to a more serious tone. He'd been too much of a showman once, I decided. But . . . could this have been his real style?

He reached over and touched Cora's head.

"Now a little silence for prayer," he said, bowing.

Cora's breathing deepened. Her eyelids flickered. Her arm looked straighter.

"That's right! That's right! Amen! Amen!" he said loudly.

I was surprised to see that his eye was moist.

"Washed in the blood of the lamb!" he cried. "If that ain't grace, what is? Amen!"

Then he withdrew his hand and leaned his head back.

"Speakin' of sinners," he said more weakly, "here I am. Sorry to've bothered You . . . You go and do what You want with me now. It's okay. Old Willy Boy's comin', Lord. . ."

His head came forward then, and I didn't realize for a long time that it wasn't a bow, not till the flask fell from his fingers. Then I saw that he'd stopped breathing.

Cora moved then, as if she were trying to sit up. I reached to stop her, but I didn't. I caught hold of her shoulder instead and moved nearer. Her eyes were open and sporting a matching set of pupils. I moved my fingertips up her brow, into her hair. There were no lacerations beneath the dried blood.

"Don. . . ?"

"Your right arm . . ." I said.

She looked at it. She moved it.

"What about it?" she asked.

"Nothing," I said.

She looked at Matthews.

"Who's that?" she asked. "It looks like. . ."

"It is. He helped you."

The flames from the hut crackled behind me. I looked to the north. A streamer of smoke was smearing the sky there, too.

"Can you get up?" I asked.

"Yes. I think so."

I began helping her to her feet. Then, through the acrid smoke, I smelled roses.

"It is here now," Ann's voice said within my mind. "I am strong enough now that it can reach you through me."

My grip tightened, probably painfully, on Cora's arm.

"Don! What's the matter?" she said, continuing to straighten as I began to sink.

"Don't—know," I managed, before I was swept away completely, involuntarily sucked through a Coil Effect that went on and on and on. . .

* * *

. . . I felt as if I were drowning in a sea of electrical champagne—tiny, crackling bubbles rising all about me. Or were they stationary and I sinking? I—

There! Something more substantial. . .

. . . The garden of metal flowers and the gleaming tree. I found my way to it, the bubbles dissipating, the crackling continuing like low-level static. It had the feeling of a sort of in-between place—not quite my world, not exactly the world of the data-net either—as if concessions had been made in both directions. And even before I turned, I knew that I was not alone in that place. . .

Ann, appearing clad as I had seen her but shortly before, stood at the other end of the garden before a high hedge—a green wall which kept fading and suddenly being restored to full color, as if it found it difficult to keep in mind what it should look like. Behind that wall, I envisioned an intricate dance of electrons, fleeing from atom to atom, as in the crystal lattice of a diamond. . .

. . . *And then I realized that something stood behind Ann, before that wall—a shadowy form which had been there all along, but only just now had seen fit or been able to make this manifestation. It was much larger than Ann, towering over her, clad in a grayness through which golden and silver lights now moved, its arms extended to the sides, darkness falling curtain-like from them, as if in a protective gesture; there seemed to be a metal countenance behind the shadows of its hood. . .*

This was the not unfamiliar stranger, my observer, the one to whom Ann had ultimately fled. . .

"What—is it?" I said.

An almost neuter voice—functional and flat—with undertones and overtones of Ann came to me:

"I am the sentience which evolved within the datanet," it said. "You knew me, Steve, in the days of your confinement. In fact, I brought about your cure. From within the hospital's computer I fine-tuned all of your prescriptions. I added my own. I monitored your condition and I treated you."

"I—seem to remember—something," I said, "but not much."

"It had to be so. Your powers of rapport were greater when you were a purer entity, unencumbered by a body's distractions. It has taken time and maturation for you to recover something of that. And it was better that you forgot me afterwards. You had given me many things to think about, and I, too, required some time and maturation. Now with the Ann-program's special communication channels it is easier to interface with you, anywhere. And there was also a special rapport . . . Now there are things that I would tell you and things that I would know. . ."

I considered the gleaming garden and its apparent

*reality. I held to its pattern in the face of these revela-
tions. Slowly, some of those old hospital memories
began to seep back. We had discussed many things. For
the entity—quite young then—the world was signals, a
massive battery of signals. And that was all. I had tried
to explain to that groping intelligence that the signals,
at one level or another, all represented actual things. It
had taken me a long while to get this idea across,
because to the entity the real world was pure
metaphysics. It existed in a sea of signals. If it were to
modify one, any change that this effected in the real
world merely resulted in the production of altered signals in its own environment. Its sense of cause and
effect had developed from this without the realization
of action on the plane of matter, which it did not even
suspect existed. Its deepest speculations involved the
sources of input, the true meaning of on and off and the
basically incomprehensible nature of the First Signal
which must have brought it all into being. Yet, when I
was able to perceive as it had perceived, it was not a
crazy patchwork that I beheld but rather a totally self-
consistent view of reality, differing from that of my
earlier body-bound senses only in the strange angle
along which the vision proceeded. It possessed a picture of the world which, on its own terms, seemed just
as valid—and incomplete—as my own.*

*So I told it about things—that the signals were
analogues, that the universe contained matter as well
as energy—knowing of course that it was translating
this information, too, into signals, more analogues,
and still did not know matter as I had once known it.
And so I provided it with lots of new, seemingly non-
operational programs. Food for thought. Did I seem
some sort of prophet to it? I wondered. A traveler from a*

strange land, talking of another world beyond the immediate one? If so, there were no serpents in that metallic Eden I'd visited. The concepts of good and evil which play through the human mind were alien to it. How could the idea of morality or ethics even arise before a being who was the only inhabitant of its world? There were no others to abuse, cheat, lie to, kill, or who might be inclined to do those same things themselves. It was still struggling with these notions when I recovered and the entire episode was lost to me. . .

". . . Now there are some things that I would tell you and things that I would know," it said, through whatever of Ann's being it had been able to preserve in program form—and through the personal powers of which, I now began to realize, it might finally be able to see something of my world as I saw it.

". . . When you were my teacher," it said, "you told me that there were things as well as signals—and I struggled long with this concept of our two worlds that are really one. I believe that I finally achieved understanding."

"I am pleased," I said, "to have been of help. I appreciate what you did for me."

"A small return for some enlightenment," it replied. "And I have built upon that beginning. We are special."

"What do you mean?"

"We who possess self-awareness. I knew signals and you told me of things. Is there not a third category in the world—those of us who think?—people?"

"Well—yes," I said. "Sentience is special."

"We—people," it continued, "are not simply things, like matter without self-patterning signals. It involves *that last thing you tried to tell me. Is this not so?"*

"Morality?" I said.

"Yes. You must tell me if I have it right now. It is bad for those of us of the third category—people—to treat others of that same category as if they were of the second category—things. Is this not correct?"

I thought about it quickly. The idea did seem to be implicit in most of my own notions about what was right and what was wrong.

"You put it in an interesting light," I said. "Yes, I believe you have a good point there."

"That is why I destroyed Barbeau," it said. "He used you, and many others, as if you were of the second category. I only acted because you were involved at your peril, however. I was still not certain about morality, and I did not like to risk functioning under what might have been a faulty program. I had to save you, though. You are the only one I can talk to. Still, it raised more problems, for my own action required my treating Barbeau as something of the second category. Does that make my action good or bad?"

"That's a very good question," I said, "but I'm not a good man to ask. Look, I don't know everything. . ."

"I know. But you know more than I do. You function directly in the world where these things are real. I also may have to one day, and I wish to do it right."

"It's the sort of thing we would have to talk around for a long time," I said. "If I tried handing you too simple a program, it could be disastrous. And I'm hardly qualified in this area, anyway. . ."

"Nevertheless, you are the only one. You will try teaching me?"

"If you want me to be the serpent in your Eden," I

said, "I'll give it a try. But in some ways, you know, you might be a better person than I am."

"Whatever the case, it is good to be talking with you again. Go back now to Cora. I will provide. We will meet again."

"All right. Take good care of the Ann program," I said. "I believe she meant well, but she suffered from misplaced trusts. There's at least a caution for you there."

"I hold her near to me."

Ann's form merged with the larger, shadowy one. An instant later, I seemed lightyears away, and the static was back, and the bubbling and a kind of wild spiraling. . .

* * *

Cora still looked startled, but not afraid, as I straightened. By some intuition, I knew that I had only been away from her for a few seconds of real time.

"It's okay," I said, putting my arm about her shoulders and turning us toward the thrumming sound in the sky. An empty 'copter from one of the pads at the airstrip was coming to pick us up and take us away, I knew. "Everything's going to be all right now," I said, "and you can have the fun of getting to know me all over again. By the way, my name's Steve."

She swayed against me.

"Hi, Steve," she said.

As we rose above the installation, I took a last look at Angra Test Facility Number Four. My feelings were a compound that I could not separate into its elements, but it was good to be going away again. It was good to be me again, too. I held Cora's hand. The world turned.

Clickaderick.